P9-EDP-424

The Masterworks of Literature Series

WILLIAM S. OSBORNE, *Editor*
Southern Connecticut State College

The Cream of the Jest

The Cream of the Jest

A Comedy of Evasion

by JAMES BRANCH CABELL

Edited for the Modern Reader by
Joseph M. Flora
UNIVERSITY OF NORTH CAROLINA

New College and University Press, Inc.
Albany, NY 12203

New Material, Introduction and Notes
by JOSEPH M. FLORA

2345678901 CCCC 8765432109

Introduction

The Cream of the Jest (1917) may be considered the finest vintage James Branch Cabell. Certainly Cabell considered it his first novel to contain his mature style. In preparing the Storisende edition for the books of the Biography of Manuel during 1927-1930, Cabell recalled: "I found all the books prior to *The Cream of the Jest* to have been written by persons who are to me, nowadays, comparative strangers. . . . only in *The Cream of the Jest* and its temporal successors had I any sense of dealing with my own work."[1] Cabell scholars have concurred—essentially—in this judgment. To Louis D. Rubin, Jr., Cabell seemed "to have arrived at just about his full style in *The Cream of the Jest,* and to have sustained it thereafter with almost no faltering."[2] And Arvin R. Wells, in his study of the development of Cabell's work, gives *The Cream of the Jest* special emphasis as a transitional comedy.[3] The most recent book about Cabell, Desmond Trannt's *James Branch Cabell: The Dream and the Reality,* places emphasis on the novel as a major statement of Cabell's philosophy.[4]

In the 1930's and 1940's when Cabell's fame had dimmed considerably, *The Cream of the Jest* remained one of the Cabell titles that literary people still read or pretended to read. For one thing, it—along with *Beyond Life*—had made its way into the Modern Library. Next to *Jurgen,* it was Cabell's most remembered book.

1. *Preface to the Past* (New York: Robert M. McBride Co., 1936), p. 205.
2. *No Place on Earth: Ellen Glasgow, James Branch Cabell and Richmond-in-Virginia* (Austin, University of Texas Quarterly, 1959), p. viii.
3. *Jesting Moses* (Gainesville: University of Florida Press, 1962), pp. 94-104.
4. *James Branch Cabell: The Dream and the Reality* (Norman: University of Oklahoma Press, 1967), pp. 192-99.

I

Aside from its literary merits, *The Cream of the Jest* has as fascinating a history as any of Cabell's books save *Jurgen*. But the truth is that for a long time Cabell was the chief believer in the romance, which he had first titled *In The Flesh*. That a new Cabell would emerge in this romance might have been predicted, for it was the first book Cabell finished after his marriage at age thirty-four to Priscilla Bradley Shepherd, a widow with five children. As Cabell acknowledged, the work was different; and he had difficulty in getting it published. Several companies had the opportunity to reject it—including the George H. Doran Company, where young Sinclair Lewis was the reader who, though he admired much of what he had read, made objections and wrote to Cabell about them. The result of this letter was a long friendship that is best chronicled in *Between Friends: Letters of James Branch Cabell and Others*. Cabell's own extra-literary fondness for *The Cream of the Jest* stemmed from the persons (like Lewis) he met because of the book's rocky reception. The novel was finally accepted by Robert M. McBride and Company, two years after its initial rejection. Far from a best seller, the novel was generally well reviewed but sometimes vehemently condemned. Most significantly for Cabell's reputation, Burton Rascoe, book-review editor of the Chicago *Tribune*, recognized its merit and began an enthusiastic campaign for Cabell. Rascoe's task was made easier after *Jurgen* was published in 1919 and was suppressed in January, 1920, and publisher McBride was ordered to stand trial for its obscenities. This notoriety was immensely helpful for the sales of *The Cream*—and for *Jurgen* after its exoneration in 1922. In 1923 John Lane published *The Cream of the Jest* in England, seven and a half years after Lane had rejected it. The Modern Library published a slightly revised version. *The Cream* had found a wide audience.

II

Yet the reader coming to Cabell for the first time might well wonder at this point just how good *The Cream* is. It will strike many as bizarre fiction, for it contains very little external action. Although its hero has dealings not only with notable personages of mythical Poictesme (Cabell's domain in medieval France) but with the famed of history, including Tiberius Caesar, Henry VIII, Shakespeare and Oliver Cromwell (to name a few), certain readers will complain that nothing happens. However, it is the conviction of Felix Bulmer Kennaston, the aging protagonist of the novel, that the only real events are mental, that success in life is much as Walter Pater defined it. In his Conclusion to *The Renaissance: Studies in Art and Poetry* (1873), Pater emphasizes that each person lives in his own world "not of objects in the solidity with which language invests them, but of impressions, unstable, flickering, inconsistent, which burn and are extinguished with our consciousness of them. . . ." He declares that it is the function of art to serve the human spirit, "to rouse, to startle it to a life of constant and eager observation." Or, as one of his most famous sentences puts it: "To burn always with this hard, gemlike flame, to maintain this ecstasy, is success in life." Kennaston's conclusion is: "Never was man brought into contact with reality save through evanescent emotions and sensations of that single moment, that infinitesimal fraction of a second, which was passing now." And so he strives to gather as many successful moments in life as possible, to live with a pure gemlike flame. And so externally, aside from a conversion to Christianity, nothing much happens to the protagonist. He lives his modestly secluded life with Kathleen, his wife, experiences a certain fame and notoriety because of the success of his fiction *Men Who Loved Alison*, has a luncheon with a distinguished political figure of his day, visits with a prelate, has an embarrassing chance meeting with a former mistress, annoys his neighbor Harrowby, and is suddenly a widower. But he dreams his dreams—dreams that are only seeming escapes from reality.

Is the novel one for a highly select company of scholars? Or may the "common reader" share in its delights? The reception depends, of course, on the reader's ability to participate in a special dream experience that may challenge fundamental assumptions about himself and the nature of all experience. The modern-day college student is sometimes put off even by *Jurgen* which was so "in" during the 1920's, and some who warm to *Jurgen* may find *The Cream* a disappointment—a disappointment certain to follow if the reader expects another *Jurgen*. Indeed, the great complexity and diversity in Cabell is mirrored by the diverse response to *The Cream*. There has always been a great deal of variance in the way even Cabell's fans have ranked his books. H. L. Mencken, for example, called *Beyond Life* "very tedious reading."[5] Yet Vincent Starrett and Vardis Fisher judged it to be of the first order.[6] Cabell said *Figures of Earth* is a favorite of many women. And critics like Oscar Cargill have damned almost all of Cabell's books although Cargill does place value on *The Cream of the Jest*.[7]

In a qualified way, then, *The Cream* has been something of a favorite. Yet the Cabell neophyte may well be cautioned that there is more than one jest in the novel, and he will need his wits about him if he is to recognize the multiple jests, for Cabell is not a writer to whom one simply surrenders. (The reader who places a mirror before the picture of the Sigil of Scoteia, upside down, will find an unexpected jest.) The emotional appeal is there and grows, but Cabell's comedy is primarily intellectual. His books often require a second and third reading. Usually they are to be ingested slowly—as certainly, I think, *The Cream of the Jest* should be.

The title of Cabell's romance has an amusing literal twist, which is revealed only near the end of the book. But that joke is hardly the whole point of the title. Another important area of meaning suggested by the title is related to narrative perspective. As a story about a middle-aged artist and his art, *The Cream of the Jest* makes fascinating comparison with James Joyce's *A Portrait of the Artist as a Young Man*, published only one year earlier (1916). Cabell's work is at

5. *Letters of H. L. Mencken*, ed. Guy J. Forgue (New York, Alfred A. Knopf, 1961), p. 162.

6. Vincent Starrett, "The Passing of James Branch Cabell," *The Double Dealer*, II (November, 1921), pp. 203-09. Vardis Fisher, *God or Caesar: The Writing of Fiction for Beginners* (Caldwell, Idaho: The Caxton Printers, 1953), pp. 54-55.

7. *Intellectual America: Ideas on the March* (New York: The Macmillan Co., 1940), pp. 495-503.

least as surprising in its narrative technique as Joyce's novel. The story of Cabell's aging artist is told by his neighbor Richard Fentor Harrowby. But Harrowby does not like Kennaston: he is annoyed at Kennaston, at his aloofness and mannerisms. He regards Kennaston, consciously, as many came to regard Cabell—as rather too precious and irrelevant. Yet the reader often forgets that Harrowby is telling the story—so omniscient is Harrowby in describing Kennaston's feelings and intentions. Kennaston himself would not have told the story very differently. Harrowby, in short, sounds like Kennaston. The Cabellian irony is that Harrowby has been so completely taken in by his author neighbor. Thus Cabell illustrates for us the fictive process. Kennaston explores a special dream world, a highly personal world—largely to escape from the imperfections of the "real" world and self; and he attempts to portray his private world in his books. When he is successful, the reader shares the dream kingdom, as Harrowby shared Kennaston's world. Richard Harrowby becomes the better self—the more imaginative self—of Felix Kennaston. Harrowby becomes Kennaston much as Kennaston becomes Horvendile, the "devil" protagonist of Kennaston's dream life.

III

A textual study of *The Cream* indicates how complete the fictive transformation in Harrowby is. The novel exists in three versions: the first of 1917; the "Kalki" edition of 1922 (the plates the Modern Library version used); and the Storisende edition of 1930. The changes Cabell made for the later versions illustrate how much he loved the act of writing. He painstakingly went through his works to prepare them for the definitive Storisende edition, the only edition he would recognize as his; and the text which Cabell would insist that the reader use is the one offered here. A special feature of the present edition is, therefore, to show the stylist at work by indicating in the appendix the changes from the first edition to the Kalki and finally the Storisende.

The changes Cabell made are instructive for purely stylistic reasons, for one of Cabell's most frequently noted traits is his graceful style. His admirers frequently praise it, and often when critics could praise Cabell for nothing else, they noted his urbane, sophisticated prose—though its ornateness came increasingly under attack. I would emphasize here, however, that Cabell's revisions—on the whole—make for greater precision and function to take us farther into Felix's world. Whereas a Hemingway might have made the prose more spare, Cabell's changes make the sentences more dream-like; he adds qualifiers more often than sentences. The punctuation changes (though some merely rectify) also function to make the pace slower, more dream-like.

In the Storisende edition Cabell uses a comma and a dash at the end of an extended qualifying phrase where most twentieth-century writers would find the dash sufficient. A Hemingway underpunctuates, not a Cabell. In the Storisende edition, Cabell has consistently added punctuation —giving, all in all, the effect of a careful, meticulous narrative by a narrator whose material does not permit him to be rushed. Similarly, we notice that Cabell in reassessing made many changes in paragraphing. Occasionally he added a paragraph to enrich a chapter; more often he broke a paragraph to form another paragraph. This device further tends to give the reader pause, and makes the final version more meditative. In his revisions Cabell added a large number of dialogue directions, such as "'Sir Guiron cried to her, in the while that the maid answered:" and "Ettarre replied pensively." He did so, not because it was difficult in the first edition to know who was speaking (as occasionally happens in Hemingway's clipped dialogue), but to add grace notes which enhance the meditative or romantic quality. Certain diction changes also further this tendency. Thus, the frequently used *however* in the first two versions becomes the more "poetic" *howsoever*. My study of the three versions of *The Cream* reveals that Cabell did not modify his main conception at all. Rather, he corrected, sought greater precision, and above all tried to make style communicate to the reader the dream quality of the experience.

Perhaps the greatest value the appendix charting Cabell's revision may have is to illustrate how totally authors (as apposed to writers) are mastered by the desire to write perfectly, how tyrannical, in fact, the Word can be. Popular writers, such as Mickey Spillane, may boast of never revising. When such a writer is finished with a book, he is finished, except to collect his royalties. He will look rather pityingly at a James Joyce or a James Branch Cabell or a Felix Kennaston. Harrowby reports that "Kennaston had come to think artistic creation in words—since marble and canvas inevitably perished—was the one, possibly, worthwhile employment of human life." The *possibility* of Harrowby's statement has a chilling effect, doubtless. And the urge to write a perfect book is doomed—as Cabell knows. But the desire to write a book with a "life beyond life" is not one easily dismissed, once accepted. Cabell was Cabell's most severe critic. Thus, the first edition of *The Cream of the Jest*—itself a product of careful writing—did not satisfy its author. Revised editions would probably gain Cabell little money. But the desire to write beautifully, to please himself made Cabell a zealous reader and reviser of his own books. Clearly, the divine muse can be fiendish.

IV

The success of any reading of *The Cream* depends upon the reader's merging into the dream-life of Kennaston, which—as I have said—is also the life of Harrowby. The flux of life between dreaming and the "real" world patterns the book. For while the quality of Kennaston's dreams gives his life the romance that the humdrum of existence mitigates against, the most moving jest of the work is the celebration of the daily life which makes the dream-life possible. Kennaston—as his Horvendile self—pursues the unattainable Ettarre, but realizes ultimately (though too late) that it is his wife Kathleen whom he loves and that this love is precisely what the dream enhances. Joe Lee Davis rightly observes that Cabell's wisdom "is not too far from Frost's in 'Birches,' "[8] for "earth is the right place for love," something that is symbolized finally in *The Cream of the Jest* by the union of the two halves of the Sigil of Scoteia.

The Cream of the Jest ends, then, not with adolescent

8. *James Branch Cabell* (New York: Twayne Publishers, Inc., 1962), p. 127.

flight—as in Joyce's *A Portrait*—but with a moving affirmation of the reality behind the dream. The novel juxtaposes not only the worlds of Felix and Harrowby (and Felix and Horvendile), but also the worlds of Felix and his practical wife. By novel's end, Kathleen has replaced Ettarre, the"witch-woman" of Felix's dreams. Felix, happy in his rich dream life, becomes at the novel's end more Kennaston, more knowing. As Felix has moved toward a more mature view of religion, he recognizes at last the utmost value of the woman in the flesh. *The Cream* is the story of Felix and Kathleen, the story of what each says.[9] Time and Death have their say in the novel, but in art and in love Felix and Kathleen move in powerful opposition to those grim realities. Cabell's original title, *In The Flesh*, emphasizes this central core of meaning. Stephen Dedalus, the immature artist of Joyce, was in his art pursuing a girl not even given a name. While she is merely the vague E. C. or Mercedes, Stephen's flight seems doomed. Cabell as well as Joyce seems to say that only when the artist has a Kathleen, a woman "in the flesh," behind his Ettarre does the artist have a chance to combat Time and Death. With those forces, we are all concerned; and because Cabell treats them so provocatively, the careful reader should find him of abiding interest.

JOSEPH M. FLORA

*The University of North Carolina
at Chapel Hill*

---

9. Perhaps even more than "Birches," Robert Frost's great poem "West-Running Brook" captures the spirit of *The Cream*, its tensions between the imaginative and the practical, between the male and the female, between life and death. Too, Frost's sonnet on the wifely ideal, "The Silken-Tent," is strikingly apt for Kathleen.

The Cream of the Jest

"It shall come to pass that instead of sweet smell there shall be stink; and instead of well set hair baldness; and instead of a stomacher a girding of sackcloth; and burning instead of beauty."

Author's Note

WE TURN now to the last of the books by Richard Fentnor Harrowby, which is "The Cream of the Jest." Meanwhile, continuing directly with the matter of "The Eagle's Shadow," I must tell you—since Harrowby has omitted this information,—that Kathleen Saumarez and Felix Kennaston were married in June 1904, to confront, as it seemed, a future of genteel poverty. But, within four months, the death of old strange Henry Kennaston, the squire of Alcluid, had changed all that gray prospect materially.

I avoid, though, any further entrance into affairs with which the Biography of Manuel's life has no close concern, and which in any case are more properly set forth in J. V. A. Froser's "Biography of Felix Kennaston." You may read therein how the elopement of Kennaston's parents, in 1867, had begun the feud between their two families,—a feud which had resulted in Kennaston's being reared by the Bulmers, without any contacts with his father's kindred,—so that, when Henry Kennaston was killed, in October 1904, his only surviving nephew acquired a competence from a person whom Felix Kennaston had not ever known or talked with, nor even seen from a distance. . . . The point here is that Felix Kennaston in his middle thirties became economically independent and was made free to devote the rest of his days to whatsoever amusements he might prefer; and that he then gave over his life to the grinding thraldom of creative writing.

— Whereby, of course, American literature was enriched with "Men who Loved Alison." . . . Of the actual and eventual worth of this romance I cannot pretend to be an unprejudiced judge. The tale seems to me one of those

many books which have profited, very dubiously indeed, by
having obtained, in one way or another, the repute of being
indecent. Such books tend to endure, but their tenure of
survival is upon depressingly twilit terms. And they make
for a most dolorous deal of dreary time-wasting. It is quite
dreadful to consider with what sad and futile perseverance
the sloppy and soporific catalogues of Rabelais, the pale
inanities of the "Heptameron," and the unendurably dull
botcheries of Boccaccio—or, for that matter, of Fielding and
of Smollett,—have been toiled through by misguided
millions in quest of these authors' rumored obscenity. . . .
But it is even more dreadful, for the ears of the fairly
honest, to hear any one of these readers protest, as they all
do invariably, that he reads not for the story's sake, but
because of the delicate art and the sparkling wit with which
the tale is told. Besides, he does get, in the way of
indecency, so very little for his trouble.

Well, and just so I doubt if "Men Who Loved Alison," in
common with a great many other modern masterpieces, does
not continue to be read to-day upon somewhat similar
grounds. As books go, it has had a long life: indeed, the tale
has survived its publication now by some twenty-one years;
and it is handsomely written, of course, in its own
over-ornate and self-conscious and clogged fashion. But I
fancy that the most of this book's readers are, here again,
those immature-minded persons who are content to put up
with the diction and with the stylistic devices for the sake of
the atoning talk about unnatural amours which, howsoever
sparsely, here and there adorns and cheers the pornoscopic
reader's laborious way.

It is, though, now that I think of it, with another book that
this Author's Note should be concerned. And my appropriate point is, rather, that with the volume now in your
hand the Biography completes the portrayal, begun in "The
Eagle's Shadow," of Felix Bulmer Kennaston and of his
adoption of the poetic attitude toward life, in the very same
Lichfield which Robert Etheridge Townsend and Colonel
Rudolph Musgrave coetaneously inhabited, and of
Kennaston's ultimate success as an Economist. Hereinafter,
then, as I have written in another place, the story of the
Biography is rounded off by presenting the poet—the *poietes*,

the "maker,"—in modern conditions; and by presenting, too, the manner of this Felix Kennaston's return into Poictesme—into that all accommodating country wherein almost anything is rather more than likely to happen,—so that, through this return, the perpetuated life of Manuel ends its seven hundred years of journeying at the exact point of its outset. The circle is thus made complete, as my last poet annihilates, through quite other means than were employed by my first poet, Madoc, the intervening twenty generations.

That is the main point. Madoc triumphed, you may remember, through the amenities of judicious punctuation. Felix Kennaston made use of wholly different methods to gain very much the same end. But Kennaston also triumphed. And the protagonist of the Biography—that protagonist being, as I have perhaps already said, the perpetuated life of Manuel,—was thus enabled, once more, to do that which seemed expected. . . . I mean, that the life of Manuel, as that life is throughout "The Cream of the Jest" embodied in Felix Bulmer Kennaston, returned into its long-lost Poictesme. I mean, that the life of Manuel thus did, in a fashion told hereinafter, conform to those ancient prophecies which had been begotten, in some part by Jurgen's essays in the imaginative, but mainly by the fond pride and faith of Dame Niafer. I mean, in brief, that this volume also narrates how "Manuel, as was his custom, did what Niafer thought best," and that it records how she had her way with him, as became a competent wife, a great long while after both of them were reputedly dead. . . . For I doubt if, in any important sense, either one of this primal pair of married lovers was truly dead, or ever will be dead. We know that the life of Manuel informed the body of Felix Kennaston: and I quite strongly suspect that Niafer survived in Kathleen Kennaston, and that Niafer continues to survive, wheresoever home-life flourishes, in the aging body of every really competent wife.

You may, likewise, hereinafter attempt in vain to read "The Lineage of Lichfield," an anomalous production which none the less appears to me not unaptly to wind up and to illustrate the long story of the wanderings of the life of Manuel, in a shape somewhere between an index and a map of that journeying. The notion of this Lineage was not mine, but was suggested to me by Lewis Galantière, as you may observe that I have honestly recorded in this brief comedy's rather long dedication. It is a dedication which comprises in itself a complete Author's Note to "The Lineage of Lichfield"; and so to this Epistle Dedicatory I now refer you, for any information which you may desire as to the latter section of the present volume.

I add merely that the Lineage was written in the summer of 1921, especially for what I imagine to have been the most easily indescribable of all American magazines, the Reviewer. The Reviewer, as published at Richmond-in-Virginia,—from a side alley in immediate antagonism to a cathedral,—was at this season in theory a fortnightly periodical, which in point of fact appeared whensoever the editors thought it might perhaps be amusing to get out another issue. In any case, the Reviewer was scheduled to become a monthly magazine in the autumn of 1921, and I had agreed to edit the first three issues in this new avatar. I did edit them, to such an extent as the vagaries of the printer permittted: and the Lineage thus made its first tri-partite appearance, in the October, November and December numbers, for 1921, of the Reviewer. It was largely due to this fact, my conscience now and then tells me, that the Reviewer was not long afterward forced to become a quarterly, and by and by a legend.

To return to "The Cream of the Jest," this tale was some while in the making. In January 1911, I think, was begun the dizain which under stars more favorable would have told about ten of Richard Harrowby's adventurings, for the most part, in the occult: but Saturn very plainly stood in the ascendant at the scheme's birth; for as these stories came into being, no one of them, save only Concerning David Jogram, met with the then present needs of any discoverable magazine. The dizain was therefore abandoned; and of the eight stories finished, some were destroyed, and the others were utilized here and there quite variously. Two of these tales, as they had been written in the spring of 1911, were in 1913 combined and rewritten, with the addition of considerable new matter, so that before 1914 had well begun to make the world safe for hypocrisy, these stories had blended into one continuous and fairly long

Comedy of Evasion, called then "In the Flesh," but a little later rechristened "The Cream of the Jest." . . . Thus did it come about that with the opening of 1915 this book set forth, in typescript, to seek the applause of enraptured multitudes.

The first of all its rejectors—acting on behalf of the George H. Doran Company, in January 1915,—was a romantic-minded and obviously young male who wrote me as to this book a wholly charming, if wholly disapproving, long letter. His objections I find to have been, severally, that my theme lacked sufficient weight to ballast more than a short story; that the portions relative to the publishing of Kennaston's novel (which turned out five years later to be uncommonly neat soothsaying) could interest no one unconnected with the world of book making; that "In the Flesh" was not verily "in the flesh," but smelt over strongly of midnight oil; and that, above all, my book failed to present in its characters a group, or even any one person, who evoked the reader's sympathy and admiration. For, as this hypercritical romanticist went on to explain— prior to subscribing himself Sincerely yours, Sinclair Lewis,—the general reading public simply cannot be induced to buy novels about unattractive and ignoble people, although the future author of "Main Street" and "Elmer Gantry" did go so far as to admit that disagreeable characters might be permissible "as villains, in naïve litera- ture which is still unashamed of melodrama."

The typescript of "In the Flesh" was soon after that, but far less colorfully, rejected by the J. B. Lippincott Company, in the month of February. For some now inexplicable reason or another it seems to have been declined by no publishing firm during March. Then, in April 1915, I paid my first visit to the offices of Robert M. McBride & Company, where yet another hitherto unheard-of young person, who signed himself Guy Holt, had been interested by the typescript of "In the Flesh" to the highly noncommittal extent of wishing to see something else by its writer. I who had four unpublished books was willing enough to oblige him. So the visit took place in due form; and thus began, upon my thirty-sixth birthday, the most staunch and the most beneficent of all my literary friendships. Moreover, McBride's, in the upshot, accepted

"The Rivet in Grandfather's Neck" for publication in the autumn of that year, and "The Certain Hour" and "From the Hidden Way" for publication in 1916: but McBride's also, quite whole-heartedly, declined to sponsor any printing of "In the Flesh."

This comedy was then put by, for some months, to make way for the publishing and the instant failure of "The Rivet in Grandfather's Neck." But in 1916 my typescript set forth once more a-traveling; and I find the itinerary to be succinct:—"Rejected by John Lane Company, in January 1916; by E. P. Dutton and Company, in March 1916; by Houghton Mifflin Company, in April 1916; by Charles Scribner's Sons, in June 1916;" The record finishes just thus, with a semicolon, which one now finds rather pathetically defiant, through its implication that this is by no means to be the end. Nevertheless, I seem thereafter, for almost an entire year, to have squandered no more currency in express charges upon this unsalable typescript. . . . The particularly disheartening part, you see, was that even at McBride's, where others of my books had met at last with editorial though not with financial favor, even there the opinion appeared unanimous with the opinions of all other publishing firms, that this especial book was wholly null and virtueless.

What happened next, I simply cannot say. I do not recall whether McBride's asked for another sight of this book or whether I again submitted it without waiting for any such invitation. Nor do I know for what reason the editorial staff of McBride's then altered its opinion as to the book now before you, beyond the fact that this changing can hardly have been caused by the firm's having meanwhile published as many as three books by me, of which all had failed forthwith and utterly. But I do know that McBride's, in April 1917, accepted "The Cream of the Jest," as the story was by this time called, just two years after they had rejected it; and I find also that the John Lane Company brought out this book in England, in 1923, some seven and a half years after the John Lane Company had rejected it. . . . The ways of all publishers, however, I discovered some while ago to be incalculable: and I do not think that any deduction can ever be drawn, through the channels of mere rationality, from any of their actions. It is perhaps the one trait which they share congenially with their authors.

The book was published, then, under its final title, "The Cream of the Jest," in September 1917, and as a marketable product fell wholly flat.

Yet its publication had results. H. L. Mencken, that unusual and indeed unique youngster who, as you may recall, had praised "The Cords of Vanity" some eight or more years earlier, now came forth, in the Smart Set, with a longish article in which "The Cream of the Jest" was favorably appraised in combination with yet another novel, quaintly entitled "The Three Black Pennys," then lately published by yet another unknown author,—a youngish Pennsylvanian, who not long after this time came to Dumbarton as a direct result of this article, so that I then met Joseph Hergesheimer, just as I a bit later met Mencken also, through virtue of having published "The Cream of the Jest."

And moreover an even younger Burton Rascoe, who, as yet in his early twenties, had very recently been made literary editor of the Chicago Tribune, chanced to be pleased by "The Cream of the Jest"; and he forthwith decided that it was a book which should not die unnoticed, at least, not in Chicago. What I take to have been the most remarkable, as it was certainly the most rambunctious, of all campaigns in the history of polite letters then opened, upon 29 December 1917, with the appearance, in the Chicago Tribune, of an article by Burton Rascoe headed Here's a Chance to Own Another First Edition. Thereafter, very much as the hapless Romans were formerly assured by the elder Cato, in his every public address upon whatsoever nominal theme, that Carthage must be destroyed, so now, upon each Saturday, week after week, all literate Chicago was assured by Burton Rascoe that Cabell must be read.

The assertion did not pass unchallenged. For at once Ben Hecht and Rupert Hughes, who, it may be remembered, ranked as well-known writers in those remote times, were moved to comment upon my various books with fervor, and with such taste as each of these then prominent littérateurs possessed, in one or another of the Chicago papers. Through the pages of the Herald-Examiner, Vincent Starrett joined

in, to commend "The Cream of the Jest": B. L. T.'s
Line-o'-Type column took up the matter of my literary
demerits, in another section of the Tribune, and in a rather
more ribald vein: whereas Keith Preston and Richard
Atwater waxed equally frank and derogatory in the Chicago
News. And then,—as when upon some field of glory the
cold draft laws have fetched face the intrepid patriots of two
nations, and the loud machine-gun then answers to the
ruthless speaking of its fellows ruthlessly,—so now did they
who shared in this debate begin replying the one to
another.

It all became quite learned, too, at the price of some
lessening in coherence and in any exact meaning. Perhaps
no one could ever have told you what all the printed rioting,
and the tumultuary paragraphs, and the ungentle name-
calling, were precisely about. But Molière, and Menander,
and Novalis, and Agathon, and Shakespeare, and Praxiteles,
and Robert W. Chambers, were all dragged somehow into
the affair during the following months of insane dispute;
and to each of these notabilities was accorded almost as
much prominence in the various critical dicta as was being
granted to me, now that Chicago had taken up polite letters
in a really serious way. For some six months, did the literati
of Chicago thus debate whether I was an unjustly neglected
author or a posturing imbecile: and the city at large must
have known, vaguely, that somebody of my name existed,
and had published a book called "The Cream of the Jest."

But the rest of America, so far as my publishers or I could
perceive, remained deplorably oblivious of both facts: "The
Cream of the Jest" had very soon appeared upon the
"Marked Down" counters in all book stores: and yet two
more years were to pass by before a book by me was to
become a more or less salable commodity, under the
transforming touch of Mr. John S. Sumner's monomania.

Meanwhile I had heard again from that stripling Sinclair
Lewis who had been the first of this book's so many
rejectors; and, since it developed that during the intervening three years his tastes had so altered that he now quite
approved of "The Cream of the Jest," therefore we met
before long, and we got on together excellently. I found
that, for my part, it was not possible to help liking and

admiring this Sinclair Lewis, even after the droll and deferential boy whom I first knew had turned out to be a world-famous genius, of an especial sort which made his first letter to me of large monetary value.

And so is it that, when I reflect that through "The Cream of the Jest" I first met Lewis, and Hergesheimer, and Mencken, and Rascoe, and Guy Holt, I can see that in the end this book became, in some sense, the most potent of all my books in its influence upon my career as a writer. This book did not get for me any general recognition. It got for me, instead, something in every way more valuable. For it was "The Cream of the Jest" which first made for me, in the seventeenth year of my writing, a few warm friends who but a little later were to fight in my behalf very nobly, and with wholly heroic tenacity. . . . That, though, is not my present theme. I have not any need here to rehearse those now ancient battlings, which indeed had not anything in particular to do with "The Cream of the Jest," and were not joined until 1920: but I have a strong need, and a never-dying urge, to record here, and to record upon every available occasion, my gratitude to all these and to yet other preservatory champions.

If few writers have met with more smug, more prurient, or more disingenuous opponents, no writer whatever, I think, has found more faithful allies. I now and then think also that, but for these allies, an almost all-important personage—I mean, that "general reader" who hereinafter becomes of a sudden aware of Felix Bulmer Kennaston in very much the same fashion wherein "the author of 'Jurgen'" also was discovered,—would perhaps have heard but little more of my later writings than in prior times this "general reader" had ever heard, during the gray and hope-deferring years before 1920, of my earlier books. And I deduce, at such seasons, that, inasmuch as it was "The Cream of the Jest" which got for me the most of these friends and valiant benefactors, I may very well be grateful to "The Cream of the Jest" likewise, upon grounds which are hardly, if at all, literary.

CONTENTS
of THE CREAM OF THE JEST

PART ONE

PART TWO

PART THREE

PART FOUR

PART FIVE

PART SIX

The Cream of the Jest

A COMEDY OF EVASION

"Le pays où je voulais aller, tu m'y as mené en songe, cette nuit, et tu étais belle . . . ah! que tu étais belle! . . . Mais, comme je n'ai aimé que ton ombre, tu me dispenseras, chère tête, de remercier ta réalité."

To

LOUISA NELSON

"at me ab amore tuo diducet
nulla senectus."

PART ONE

**Which touches upon Poictesme without
settling in the province**

"Give place, fair ladies, and begone,
Ere pride hath had a fall!
For here at hand approacheth one
Whose grace doth stain you all.

"Ettarre is well compared
Unto the Phoenix kind,
Whose like was never seen or heard,
That any man can find."

CHAPTER 1

Palliation of the Gambit

MUCH HAS BEEN WRITTEN critically about Felix Kennaston since the disappearance of his singular personality from the field of contemporary writers; and Mr. Froser's *Biography* contains all it is necessary to know as to the facts of Kennaston's life. Yet most readers of the *Biography*, I think, must have felt that the great change in Kennaston no long while after he "came to forty year"—this sudden, almost unparalleled, conversion of a talent for tolerable verse into the full-fledged genius of *Men Who Loved Alison*,—stays, after all, unexplained. . . .

Hereinafter you have Kennaston's own explanation. I do not know but that in hunting down one enigma it raises a bevy; but it, at worst, tells from his standpoint honestly how this changing came about.

You are to remember that the tale is pieced together, in part from social knowledge of the man, and in part from the notes I made as to what Felix Kennaston in person told me, bit by bit, a year or two after events the tale commemorates. I had known the Kennastons for some while, with that continual shallow intimacy into which chance forces most country people with their near neighbors, before Kennaston ever spoke of—as he called the thing—the sigil. And, even then, it was as if with negligence he spoke, telling of what happened—or had appeared to happen,—and answering my questions, with simply dumbfounding personal unconcern. It all seemed indescribably indecent: and I marveled no little, I can remember, as I took my notes. . . .

Now I can understand it was just that his standard of values was no longer ours nor really human. You see—it hardly matters through how dependable an agency, —Kennaston no longer thought of himself as a man of flesh-and-blood moving about a world of his compeers. Or, at least, that especial aspect of his existence was to him no longer a phase of any particular importance.

But to tell of his thoughts, is to anticipate. Hereinafter you have them full measure and, such as it is, his story. You must permit that I begin it in my own way, with what may to you at first seem dream-stuff. So I commence at Storisende, in the world's youth, when the fourth Count Emmerick, gray Manuel's not over-glorious son, was again ruling in Poictesme, now that the rebellion of Maugis d'Aigremont appeared virtually at an end. . . . For with such roundabout gambits alone can some of us approach—as one fancy begets another, if you will,—to proud assurance that life is not a blind and aimless business; not all a hopeless waste and confusion; and that we ourselves may (by and by) be strong and excellent and wise.

Such, in any event, is the road that Kennaston took, and such the goal to which he was conducted. So, with that goal in view, I also begin where he began, and follow whither the dream led him. Meanwhile, I can but entreat you to remember it is only by preserving faith in human dreams that we may, after all, perhaps some day make them come true.

RICHARD FENTNOR HARROWBY

Montevideo
14 *April* 1917

CHAPTER 2

Introduces the Ageless Woman

THE TALE TELLS how Count Emmerick planned a notable marriage-feast for his sister La Beale Ettarre and Sir Guiron des Rocques. The tale relates that, in honor of this wedding, came from Nacumera, far oversea, Count Emmerick's elder sister Dame Melicent and her husband the Comte de la Forêt, with an outlandish retinue of pagan slaves that caused great wonder. All Poictesme took holiday. The tale narrates how from Naimes to Lisuarte, and in the wild hill-country back of Perdigon, knights made ready for the tournament, traveling toward Storisende in gay silken garments such as were suited to these new times of peace. The highways in those parts shone with warriors, riding in companies of six or eight, wearing mantles worked in gold, and mounted upon valuable horses that glittered with new bits and housings. And the tale tells, also, how they came with horns sounding before them.

Ettarre watched from the turrets of Storisende, pensively. Yet she was happy in these days. "Indeed, there is now very little left this side of heaven for you to desire, madame," said Horvendile the clerk, who stood beside her at his service.

"No, there is nothing now which troubles me, Horvendile, save the thought of Maugis d'Aigremont. I cannot ever be sure of happiness so long as that man lives."

"So, so!" says Horvendile,—"ah, yes, a master-villain, that! He is foiled for the present, and in hiding, nobody knows where; but I, too, would not wonder should he be contriving some new knavery. Say what you may, madame, I cannot but commend his persistency, howsoever base be his motives; and in the forest of Bovion, where I rescued you from his clutches, the miscreant spoke with a hellish gusto that I could have found it in my heart to admire."

Ettarre had never any liking for this half-scoffing kind of talk, to which the clerk was deplorably prone. "You speak very strangely at times, Horvendile. Wickedness cannot ever be admirable; and to praise it, even in jest, cannot but be displeasing to the Author of us all."

"Eh, madame, I am not so sure of that. Certainly, the Author of those folk who have figured thus far in your history has not devoted His talents to creating perfect people."

She wondered at such foolish speaking, and she showed as much in the big blue eyes which had troubled so many men's sleep. "Since time began, there has lived no nobler person or more constant lover than my lord Guiron."

"Oh, yes, Sir Guiron, I grant you, is very nearly immaculate," said Horvendile; and he yawned.

To that, Ettarre replied: "My friend, you have always served him faithfully. We two cannot ever forget how much we have owed in the past to your quick wits and shrewd devices. Yet now your manner troubles me."

Dame Ettarre spoke the truth, for, knowing the man to be unhappy,—and suspecting the reason of his unhappiness, too,—she would have comforted him; but Horvendile was not in a confiding mood. Whimsically he says:

"Rather, it is I who am troubled, madame. For envy possesses me, and a faint teasing weariness also possesses me, because I am not as Sir Guiron, and never can be. Look you, they prepare your wedding-feast now, your former sorrows are stingless; and to me, who have served you through hard seasons of adversity, it is as if I had been reading some romance, and had come now to the last page. Already you two grow shadowy; and already I incline to rank Sir Guiron and you, madame, with Arnaud and Fregonde, with Palmerin and Polinarda, with Gui and Floripas,—with that fair throng of noted lovers whose innocuous mishaps we follow with pleasant agitation, and whom, when all is done, we dismiss to eternal happiness, in the while that we, with smiling incredulity, get back to our workaday world. For it is necessary now that I return to my own country, and there I shall not ever see you any more."

Ettarre, in common with the countryside, knew the man hopelessly loved her; and she pitied him today beyond wording. Happiness is a famed breeder of magnanimity. "My poor friend, we must get you a wife. Are there no women in your country?"

"Ah, but there is never any woman in one's own country whom one can love, madame," replies Horvendile shrewdly. "For love, I take it, must look toward something not quite accessible, something not quite understood. Now, I have been so unfortunate as to find the women of my country lacking in reticence. I know their opinions concerning everything,—touching God and God's private intentions, and touching me, and the people across the road,—and I know, too, what is the good faith and the loving tenderness and the never-sleeping jealousy of these women, and how these women's clothes are adjusted, and what they eat for breakfast, and what men have kissed them: there is no room for illusion anywhere. Nay, more: I am familiar with the mothers of these women, and in them I see quite plainly what these women will be some twenty years from this morning; there is not even room for hope. Ah, no, madame; the women of my country are the pleasantest of comrades, and the helpfullest of wives: but I cannot conceal it from myself that, after all, they are only human beings; and therefore it has not ever been possible for me to love any one of them."

"And am I not, then, a human being, poor Horvendile?"

There was a tinge of mischief in the query; but beauty very often makes for lightheadedness, both in her that has and in him that views it; nor between Ind and Thule was there any lovelier maid than Ettarre. Smiling she awaited his answer; the sunlight glorified each delicate clarity of color in her fair face, and upon her breast gleamed the broken sigil of Scoteia, that famed talisman which never left her person.

"And am I not, then, a human being?" says she. . . .

Gravely Horvendile answered: "Not in my eyes, madame. For you embody all that I was ever able to conceive of beauty and fearlessness and strange purity. Therefore it is evident I do not see in you merely Count Emmerick's third sister, but, instead, that ageless, lovable and loving woman long worshiped and sought everywhere in vain by all poets."

"But," said Ettarre, "but I had thought poets were famous for their inconstancy. It is remarkable hearing that, to the contrary, they have all loved steadfastly the same woman; and, in any case, I question how, without suspecting it, I could have been that woman."

Horvendile meditated for a while, and then said: "Assuredly, it was you of whom blind Homer dreamed, comforting endless night with visions of your beauty, as you sat in a bright fragrant vaulted chamber weaving at a mighty loom, and embroidering on tapestry the battles men were waging about Troy because of your beauty; and very certainly it was to you that Hermes came over fields of violets and parsley, where you sang magic rhymes, sheltered by an island cavern, in which cedar and citron-wood were burning,—and, calling you Calypso, bade you release Odysseus from the spell of your beauty. Sophocles, too, saw you bearing an ewer of bronze, and treading gingerly among gashed lamentable corpses, lest your loved dead be dishonored; and Sophocles called you Antigone, praising your valor and your beauty. And when men named you Bombyca, Theocritus also sang of your grave drowsy voice and your feet carven of ivory, and of your tender heart and all your honey-pale sweet beauty."

Ettarre replied, "I do not remember any of these troubadours you speak of, my poor Horvendile; but I am very certain that if they were poets they, also, must in their time have talked a great deal of nonsense."

"And as Mark's Queen," says Horvendile, intent on his conceit, "you strayed with Tristran in the sunlit glades of Morois, that high forest, where many birds sang full-throated in the new light of spring; as Medeia you fled from Colchis; and as Esclairmonde you delivered Huon from the sardonic close wiles of heathenry, which to you seemed childish. All poets have had these fitful glimpses of you, Ettarre, and of that perfect beauty which is full of troubling reticences, and so, is somehow touched with something sinister. Now all these things I likewise see in you, Ettarre; and therefore, for my own sanity's sake, I dare not concede that you are a human being."

The clerk was very much in earnest. Ettarre granted that, insane as his talk seemed to her; and the patient yearning in his eyes was not displeasing to Ettarre. Her hand touched his cheek, quickly and lightly, like the brush of a bird's wing.

"My poor Horvendile, you are in love with fantasies. There was never any lady such as you dream of."

Then she left him.

But Horvendile remained at the parapet, peering out over broad rolling uplands.

CHAPTER **3**

Wherein a Clerk Appraises a Fair Country

HORVENDILE peered out over broad rolling uplands. . . . He viewed a noble country, good to live in, rich with grain and metal, embowered with tall forests, and watered by pleasant streams. Walled cities it had, and castles crowned its eminences. Very far beneath Horvendile the leaded roofs of these fortresses glittered in sunlight, for Storisende guarded the loftiest part of all inhabited Poictesme.

And the people of this land—from its lords of the high, the low, and the middle justice, to the sturdy whining beggars at its cathedral doors,—were not all unworthy of this fair realm. Undoubtedly, it was a land, as Horvendile whimsically reflected, wherein human nature kept its first dignity and strength; and wherein human passions were never in a poor way to find expression with adequate speech and action.

Now, from the field below, a lark rose singing joyously. Straight into the air it rose, and was lost in the sun's growing brilliance; but you could hear its singing; and then, as suddenly, the bird dropped to earth. No poet could resist embroidery on such a text.

Began Horvendile straightway: *"Quan vey la laudeta mover"*—or in other wording:

"When I behold the skylark move in perfect joy toward its love the sun, when I behold the skylark, growing drunk with joy, forget the use of wings, so that it topples from the height of heaven, I envy the bird's fate. I, too, would taste that ruinous mad moment of communion, there in heaven, and my heart dissolves in longing.

"Ailas! how little do I know of love!—I, who was once deluded by the conceit that I was all-wise in love. For I am unable to put aside desire for a woman whom I must always love in vain. She has bereft me of hope. She has robbed me of my heart, of herself, and of all joy in the world, and she has left me nothing save dreams and regrets.

"Never have I been able to recover my full senses since that moment when she first permitted me to see myself mirrored in her bright eyes. Hey, fatal mirrors! which flattered me too much! for I have sighed ever since I beheld my image in you. Your shining is a ruining fire. I have lost myself in you, like Narcissus in his fountain."

Thus he lamented, standing alone among the turrets of Storisende. Now a troop of jongleurs was approaching the castle,—gay dolls, jerked by invisible wires, the vagabonds seemed to be, from this height.

"More merry-makers for the marriage-feast. We must spare no appropriate ceremony. And yonder Count Emmerick is ordering the major-domo to prepare peacocks stuffed with beccaficoes, and a pastry builded like a palace. Hah, my beautiful fantastic little people, that I love and play with, and dispose of just as I please, it is time your master shift another puppet."

So Horvendile descended, still poetizing: *"Pus ab mi dons no m pot valer"*—or in other wording:

"Since nothing will avail to move my lady,—not prayers or righteous claims or mercy,—and she desires my homage now no longer, I shall have nothing more to say of love. I must renounce love, and abjure it utterly. I must regard her whom I love as one no longer living. I must, in fine, do that which I prepare to do; and afterward I must depart into eternal exile."

CHAPTER **4**

Of the Double-Dealer's Traffic with a Knave

HORVENDILE left the fortress, and came presently to Maugis d'Aigremont. Horvendile got speech with this brigand where he awaited encamped in the hill-country of Perdigon, loth to leave Storisende since it held Ettarre whom he so much desired, but with too few adherents to venture an attack.

Maugis sprawled listless in his chair, wrapped in a mantle of soiled and faded green stuff, as though he were cold. In his hand was a naked sword, with which moodily he was prodding the torn papers scattered about him. He did not move at all, but his somber eyes lifted.

"What do you plan now, Horvendile?"

"Treachery, messire."

"It is the only weapon of you scribblers," Maugis answered. "How will it serve me?"

Then Horvendile spoke. Maugis sat listening. Above the swordhilt the thumb of one hand was stroking the knuckles of the other carefully. His lean and sallow face stayed changeless.

Says Maugis: "It is a bold stroke—yes. But how do I know it is not some trap for me?"

Horvendile shrugged, and asked, "Have I not served you constantly in the past, messire?"

"You have suggested makeshifts, very certainly. . . . And to a pretty pass they have brought me! Here I roost like a starved buzzard, with no recreation except upon clear forenoons to look at the towers of Storisende."

"Meanwhile, at Storisende," said Horvendile, "Ettarre prepares to marry Sir Guiron."

"I think of that. . . . She is very beautiful, is she not, Horvendile? And she loves this stately kindly fool who carries his fair head so high and has no reason to hide anything from her. Yes, she is very beautiful, being created perfect by divine malice, in order that she might be the ruin of men. So I loved her: and she did not love me, because I was not worthy of her love. And Guiron is in all things worthy of her. I cannot ever pardon him that."

Horvendile said then, "And I am pointing out a way, messire, by which you may reasonably hope to deal with Sir Guiron—ho, and with the Counts Emmerick and Perion, and Heitman Michael, and with Ettarre also,—precisely as you elect."

Now Maugis spoke wearily. "I must trust you, I suppose. But I have no lively faith in my judgments nowadays. I have played fast and loose with too many men, and the stench of their blood is in my nostrils, drugging me. I move in a half-sleep, and people's talking seems remote and foolish. I can think clearly only when I think of how tender is the flesh of Ettarre. Heh, a lovely flashing peril allures me, through these days of fog, and I must trust you. Death is ugly, I know; but life is ugly too, and all my deeds are strange to me."

The clerk was oddly moved. "Do you not know I love you as I never loved Guiron?"

"How can I tell? You are an outlander. Your ways are not our ways," says the brigand moodily. "And what have I to do with love?"

"You will talk otherwise when you drink in the count's seat, with Ettarre upon your knee," Horvendile considered. "Observe, I do not promise you success! Yet I would have you remember it was by very much this same device that Count Perion won the sister of Ettarre."

"Heh, if we fail," replies Maugis, "I shall at least have done with remembering. . . ." Then they settled details of the business in hand.

Thus Horvendile returned to Storisende before twilight had thickened into nightfall. He came thus to a place different in all things from the haggard outlaw's camp, for Count Emmerick held that night a noble revel. There was gay talk and jest and dancing, with all other mirth men could devise.

The barons of Poictesme had well-nigh lost the knack of dancing, during the twelve years of never-ending warfare which had been stirred up by the lust and greed of Maugis d'Aigremont: but to-night all trouble seemed to have departed from Storisende; and these warriors merrily returned to the sports of their youth.

CHAPTER 5

How the Double-Dealer Was of Two Minds

IT WAS deep silent night when Horvendile came into the room where Ettarre slept. "Out, out!" cried Horvendile. "Let us have more light here, so that men may see the beauty men die for!" He went with a torch from lamp to lamp, kindling them all.

Ettarre stood between the bed-curtains, which were green hangings worked with birds and beasts of the field, each in his proper colors. The girl was robed in white; and upon her breast gleamed the broken sigil of Scoteia, that famed talisman which never left her person. She wore a scarlet girdle about her middle, and her loosened yellow hair fell heavy about her. Her fine proud face questioned the clerk in silence, without any trace of fear.

"We must wait now," says Horvendile, "wait patiently for that which is to follow. For while the folk of Storisende slept—while your fair, favored lover slept, Ettarre, and your stout brothers Emmerick and Perion slept, and all persons who are your servitors and well-wishers slept,—I, I, the puppet-shifter, have admitted Maugis d'Aigremont and his men into this castle. They are at work now, hammer-and-tongs, to decide who shall be master of Storisende and of you."

Her first speech you would have found odd at such a time. "But, oh, it was not you who betrayed us, Horvendile, —not you whom Guiron trusted!"

"You forget," he returned, "that I, who am without any hope to win you, must attempt to view the squabbling of your other lovers without bias. It is the custom of omnipotence to do that, Ettarre. I have given Maugis d'Aigremont an equal chance with Sir Guiron. It is the custom of omnipotence to do that also, Ettarre. You will remember the tale was trite even in Job's far time that the sweetmeats of life do not invariably fall to immaculate people."

Then, as if on a sudden, Dame Ettarre seemed to understand that the clerk's brain had been turned through his hopeless love for her. She wondered, dizzily, how she could have stayed blind to his insanity this long, recollecting the inconsequence of his acts and speeches in the past; but matters of heavier urgency were at hand. Here, with this apparent madman, she was on perilous ground; but now had arisen a hideous contention without: and the shrieks there, and the clash of metal there, spoke with rude eloquence of company even less desirable.

"Heaven will defend the right!" Ettarre said bravely.

Horvendile replied: "I am not sure that Heaven has any finger in this pie. An arras hides all. It will lift presently, and either Good or Evil, either Guiron or Maugis, will come through that arras as your master. I am not certain, as yet, which one I shall permit to enter; and the matter rests with me, Ettarre."

"Heaven will defend the right!" Ettarre said bravely.

And at that the arras quivered and heaved, so that its heavy embroideries were converted into a welter of shimmering gold, bright in the glare of many lamps, sparkling like the ocean's waters at sunset; and Horvendile and Ettarre saw nothing else there for a breathless moment, which seemed to last for a great while. Then, parting, the arras yielded up Maugis d'Aigremont.

Horvendile chuckled.

CHAPTER **6**

Treats of Maugis
d'Aigremont's Pottage

MAUGIS came forward, his eyes fixed hungrily upon Ettarre. "So a long struggle ends," he said, very quiet. "There is no virtue left, Ettarre, save patience."

The girl said: "While life remains I shall not cease to shriek out your villainy. O God, men have let Guiron die!" she wailed.

"I will cause you to forget that death is dreadful, Ettarre!"

"I need no teacher now. . . . And so, Guiron is dead and I yet live! I had not thought that would be possible." She whispered this. "Give me your sword, Maugis, for just a little while, and then I will not hate you any longer."

The man said, with dreary patience: "Yes, you would die rather than endure my touch. And through my desire of you I have been stripped of wealth and joy and honor, and even of hope; through my desire of you I have held much filthy traffic, with treachery and theft and murder, traffic such as my soul loathed: and to no avail! Yes, I have been guilty of many wickednesses, as men estimate these matters; and yet, I swear to you, I seem to myself to be still that boy with whom you used to play, when you too were a child, Ettarre, and did not hate me. Heh, it is very strange how affairs fall out in this world of ours, so that a man may discern no aim or purpose anywhere!"

"Yet it is all foreplanned, Maugis." Horvendile spoke thus.

"And to what end have you ensnared me, Horvendile?" says Maugis, turning wearily. "For the attack on Storisende has failed, and I am dying of many wounds. See how I bleed! Guiron and Michael and Perion and all their men are hunting me everywhere beyond that arras, and I am frightened, Horvendile,—even I, who was Maugis, am frightened!—lest any of them find me too soon. I desire now only to die untroubled. Oh, Horvendile, in an ill hour I trusted you!"

As knave and madman, Ettarre saw the double-dealer and his dupe confront each other. In the haggard face of Maugis, no longer evil, showed only puzzled lassitude. In the hand of Horvendile a dagger glittered; and his face was pensive, as he replied:

"My poor Maugis, it is not yet time I make my dealings plain to you. It suffices that you have served my turn, Maugis, and that of you I have no need any longer. You must die, now, Maugis."

Ettarre feared this frozen madman, she who by ordinary was fearless. Ettarre turned away her face, so that she might not see the two men grapple. Without, the uproar continued,—for a long while, it seemed. When she looked again it was, by some great wonder-working, to meet Guiron's eyes and Guiron's lips.

CHAPTER 7

Journeys End: With the Customary Unmasking

MY LOVE, Ettarre, they have not harmed you?" Sir Guiron cried to her, in the while that the maid answered: "None has harmed me, Guiron. Oh, and you?"

"Maugis is dead," the tall warrior said joyously. "See, here he lies, slain by brave Horvendile. And the rogues who followed Maugis are all killed or fled. Our woes are at an end, dear love."

Then Ettarre saw that Horvendile indeed waited beside the dead body of Maugis d'Aigremont. And the clerk remained wholly motionless while Ettarre spoke. She told Guiron of this Horvendile's baleful work.

Sir Guiron then said, "Is this true speech, Horvendile?"

"It is quite true I have done all these things, messire," Horvendile answered, without moving, even now.

"And with what purpose?" said Sir Guiron, very sadly; for to him too it seemed certain that such senseless treachery could not spring from anything but madness, and he had hitherto esteemed Horvendile as a competent and a quite useful servant.

"I will tell you," Horvendile replied, "though I much fear you will not understand—" He meditated. He shook his red curls, smilingly. "Indeed, how is it possible for me to make you understand? Well, I blurt out the truth. There was once in a land very far away from this land—in my country—a writer of romances. And once he constructed a romance which, after a hackneyed custom of my country, he pretended to translate from an old manuscript written by an ancient clerk—called Horvendile. It told of Horvendile's part in the love business between Sir Guiron des Rocques and La Beale Ettarre. I am that maker of romance. This room, this castle, all the broad rolling countryside without, is but a portion of my dream, and these places have no existence save in my fancies. And you, messire,—and you also, madame,—and dead Maugis here, and all the others who seemed so real to me, are but the puppets I have fashioned and have shifted, for a tale's sake, in that romance which now draws near to its ending."

He paused; and Sir Guiron sighed. "My poor Horvendile!" was all he said.

"It is not possible for you to believe me, of course," the clerk assented. "And it may be that I, too, am only a figment of some greater dream, in just such case as yours, and that I, too, cannot understand. It may be the very cream of the jest that my country is no more real than Storisende. How could I judge if I, too, were a puppet? It is a thought which often troubles me. . . ."

Horvendile deliberated, then spoke more briskly. "At all events, I must return now to my own country, which I do not love as I love this bright fantastic Poictesme that I created—or seemed to create,—and wherein I was—or seemed to be—omnipotent."

Horvendile drew a deep breath; and he looked downward at the corpse he had bereft of pride and daring and of agility. "Farewell, Maugis! It would be indecorous, above all in omnipotence, to express anything save abhorrence toward you: yet I delighted in you as you lived and moved; and it was not because of displeasure with you that I brought you to disaster. Hence, also, one might evolve a heady analogue. . . ."

Guiron was wondering what he might do in accord with honor and with clemency. He did not stir as Horvendile came nearer. The clerk showed very pitiful and mean beside this stately champion in full armor, all shining metal, save for a surcoat of rose-colored stuff irregularly worked with crescents of silver.

"Farewell, Sir Guiron!" Horvendile then said. "There are no men like you in my country. I have found you difficult to manage; and I may confess now that I kept you so long imprisoned at Caer Idryn, and caused you to spend so many chapters oversea in heathendom, mainly in order that I might here weave out my romance untroubled by your disconcerting and rather wooden perfection. But you are not the person to suspect ill of your creator. You are all that I once meant to be, Guiron, you are all that I have forgotten how to be; and for a dead boy's sake I have loved you even when I shrugged at your so many chivalrous virtues."

"Listen, poor wretch!" Sir Guiron answered, sternly; "you have this night done horrible mischief, you have caused the death of many estimable persons. Yet I have thriven by your aid; and I know that Heaven, through Heaven's inscrutable wisdom, has smitten you with madness. That stair leads to the postern on the east side of the castle. Go forth from Storisende as quickly as you may, whilst none save us knows of your double-dealings. It may be that I am doing great wrong; but I cannot forget I have twice owed my life to you. If I must err at all hazards, I prefer to err upon the side of gratitude and mercy."

"That is said very like you," Horvendile replied. "Eh, it was not for nothing I endowed you with sky-towering magnanimity. Assuredly, I go, messire. And so farewell, Ettarre!"

Long and very long Horvendile gazed upon the maiden. "There is no woman like you in my country, Ettarre. I can find no woman anywhere resembling you whom dreams alone may win to. It is a little thing to say that I have loved you; it is a bitter thing to know that I must live among, and pursue, and win, those other women."

"My poor Horvendile," she answered, very lovely in her compassion, "you are in love with fantasies."

He held her hand, touching her for the last time; and he trembled. "Yes, I am in love with my fantasies, Ettarre; and, none the less, I must return into my own country."

As he considered the future, in the man's face showed only puzzled lassitude; and you saw therein a quaint resemblance to Maugis d'Aigremont. "I find my country an inadequate place in which to live," says Horvendile. "Oh, many persons live there happily enough! or, at worst, they seem to find the prizes and the applause of my country worth striving for whole-heartedly. But there is that in some of us which gets no exercise there; and we struggle blindly, with impotent yearning, to gain outlet for great powers which we know that we possess, even though we do not know their names. And so, we dreamers wander at adventure to Storisende—oh, and into more perilous realms sometimes!—in search of a life that will find employment for every faculty we have. For life in my country does not engross us utterly. We dreamers waste there at loose ends, waste futilely. All which we can ever see and hear and touch there, we dreamers dimly know, is at best but a portion of the truth, and is possibly not true at all. Oh, yes! it may be that we are not sane; could we be sure of that, it would be a comfort. But, as it is, we dreamers only know that life in my country does not content us, and never can content us. So we struggle, for a tiny dear-bought while, into other and fairer-seeming lands in search of—we know not what! And, after a little"—he relinquished the maiden's hands, he spread out his own hands, shrugging,—"after a little, we must go back into my country and live there as best we may."

A whimsical wise smile now visited Ettarre's lips. Her hands went to her breast, and presently one half of the broken sigil of Scoteia lay in Horvendile's hand.

"You will not always abide in your own country,

Horvendile. Some day you will return to us at Storisende. The sign of the Dark Goddess will prove your safe-conduct then if Guiron and I be yet alive."

Horvendile raised to his mouth the talisman warmed by contact with her sweet flesh. "It may be you will not live for a great while," he says; "but that will befall through no lack of loving pains on your creator's part."

Then Horvendile left them. In the dark passageway he did not pause, but he glanced back at Guiron and Ettarre for the while of a heart-beat.

Guiron and Ettarre had forgotten his existence. Hand in hand they stood in the bright room, young, beautiful and glad. Silently their lips met. The two had put away all sorrow. They did not know of the gray Norns' decreeing as to Ettarre, nor of that long imprisonment which awaited her in the Waste Beyond the Moon, nor of that ruining which was to come of her loveliness in yet other centuries thereafter.

Horvendile closed the door, and so left Storisende. Without, he came into a lonely quiet-colored world already expectant of dawn's occupancy. Already the tree trunks eastward showed like the black bars of a grate. Thus he walked in twilight, carrying away from Storisende one half of the sigil of Scoteia. . . .

PART TWO

Which deals with, among other unsatisfying matters, Lichfield

"Whate'er she be—
That inaccessible She
That doth command my heart and me:

"Till that divine
Idea take a shrine
Of crystal flesh, through which to shine:

"Let her full glory,
My fancies, fly before ye;
Be ye my fictions—but her story."

CHAPTER 8

Of a Trifle Found
in Twilight

THUS he walked in twilight, regretful that he must return to his own country, and live another life, and bear another name, than that of Horvendile. . . . It was droll that in his own country he should be called Felix, since Felix meant "happy"; and assuredly he was not pre-eminently happy there.

At least he had ended the love business of Ettarre and Guiron happily, howsoever droll the necessitated makeshifts might have been. . . . He had very certainly introduced the god in the car, against Horatian admonition, had wound up affairs with a sort of transformation scene. . . . It was, perhaps, at once too hackneyed and too odd an ending to be aesthetically satisfactory, after all. . . . Why, beyond doubt it was. He shrugged his impatience.

"Yet—what a true ending it would be!" he reflected.

He was still walking in twilight—for the time was approaching sunset,—in the gardens of Alcluid. He must devise another ending for this high-hearted story of Guiron and Ettarre.

Felix Kennaston smiled a little over the thought of ending the romance with such topsy-turvy anticlimaxes as his woolgathering wits had blundered into; and, stooping, picked up a shining bit of metal that lay beside the pathway. He was conscious of a vague notion he had just dropped this bit of metal.

"It is droll how we great geniuses instinctively plagiarize," he reflected. "I must have seen this a half-hour ago, when I was walking up and down planning my final chapters. And so, I wove it into the tale as a breast-

51

ornament for Ettarre, without ever consciously seeing the
thing at all. Then, presto! I awake and find it growing dark,
with me lackadaisically astray in the twilight with this
picked-up piece of trash, just as I imagined Horvendile
walking out of the castle of Storisende carrying much such a
jigumicrank. Oh, yes, the processes of inspiration are as
irrational as if all poets took after their mothers."

This bit of metal, Kennaston afterward ascertained, was
almost an exact half of a disk, not quite three inches in
diameter, which somehow had been broken or cut in two. It
was of burnished metal—lead, he thought,—about a six-
teenth of an inch in thickness; and its single notable feature
was the tiny characters with which one surface was
inscribed.

Later Felix Kennaston was destined to puzzle over his
inability to recollect what motive prompted him to slip this
glittering trifle into his pocket. A trifle was all that it
seemed then. He always remembered quite clearly how it
sparkled in the abating glare of that day's portentous sunset;
and how the tree-trunks westward showed like the black
bars of a grate, as he walked slowly through the gardens of
Alcluid. Alcluid, be it explained, was the queer name with
which Felix Kennaston's progenitors had seen fit to christen
their fine country home near Lichfield.

CHAPTER 9

Beyond Use and Wont
Fares the Road to Storisende

KENNASTON was to recall, also, that on this evening he
dined alone with his wife, sharing a taciturn meal. He and
Kathleen talked of very little, now, save the existent day's
small happenings, such as having seen So-and-so, and of
So-and-so's having said this-or-that, as Kennaston reflected

in the solitude of the library. But soon he was contentedly laboring upon the book he had always intended to write some day.

Off and on, in common with most high-school graduates, Felix Kennaston had been an "intending contributor" to various magazines, spasmodically bartering his postage-stamps for courteously-worded rejection-slips. Then, too, in the old days before his marriage, when Kennaston had come so near to capturing Margaret Hugonin and her big fortune, the heiress had paid for the printing of *The King's Quest* and its companion enterprises in rhyme, as well as the prose *Defence of Ignorance*,—wide-margined specimens of the far-fetched decadence then in vogue, and the idol of Kennaston's youth, when he had seriously essayed the parlor-tricks of "stylists."

And it was once a familiar story how Marian Winwood got revenge on Felix Kennaston, when he married Kathleen Saumarez, by publishing, in a transparent guise of fiction, all the love-letters he had written Miss Winwood; so that Kennaston might also have claimed to be generally recognized as the actual author of her *Epistles of Ananias*, which, not long before this time, had created some literary stir.

But this book was to be different from any of his previous compositions. To paraphrase Felix Kennaston's own words (as recorded in the "Colophon" to *Men Who Loved Alison*), he had determined in this story lovingly to deal with an epoch and a society, and even a geography, whose comeliness had escaped the wear-and-tear of ever actually existing. He had attempted a jaunt into that "happy, harmless Fableland" which is bounded by Avalon and Phaeacia and Sea-coast Bohemia, and the contiguous forests of Arden and Broceliande, and on the west of course by the Hesperides, because he believed this country to be the one possible setting for a really satisfactory novel. Kennaston was completing, in fine, *The Audit at Storisende*,—or, rather, *Men Who Loved Alison*, as the book came afterward to be called.

Competent critics in plenty have shrugged over Kennaston's cliché of pretending that the romance is "re-told" from an ancient manuscript. But to Kennaston the clerk

Horvendile, the fictitious first writer of the chronicle and eye-witness of its events, was necessary. No doubt it handicapped the story's progress, so to contrive matters that one subsidiary character should invariably be at hand when important doings were in execution, and should be taken more or less into everyone's confidence,—but then, somehow, it made the tale seem real.

For in the writing it all seemed perfectly real to Felix Kennaston. His life was rather barren of motive now. In remoter times, when he had wandered impecuniously from one adventure to another, sponging without hesitancy upon such wealthy people as his chatter amused, there had always been exquisite girls to make love to,—such girls as the younger generation did not produce,—and the ever-present problem of whence was to come the fares for to-morrow's hansoms, in which the younger generation did not ride. For now hansom cabs were wellnigh as uncommon as bicycles or sedan-chairs, he owned two motors, and, by the drollest turn, had money in four banks. As recreation went, he and Kathleen had in Lichfield their round of decorous social duties; and there was nothing else to potter with save the writing. And a little by a little the life he wrote of came to seem to Felix Kennaston more real, and far more vital, than did the life his body was shuffling through aimlessly.

This was not the first time that Kennaston had written of Ettarre and Horvendile: for the *King's Quest*, of course, tells all about that ruining which this evasive pair contrived for King Alfgar, in somewhat stodgy Spenserian verse. But Kennaston now understood this Horvendile more completely. . . . And so, as Horvendile, he now lived among such gallant circumstances as he had always vaguely hoped his real life might provide by and by.

This Horvendile, coming unintelligibly to Storisende, and witnessing there the long combat between Sir Guiron des Rocques and Maugis d'Aigremont for possession of La Beale Alison,—as Kennaston's heroine is called, of course, in the printed book,—this Horvendile now seems to us no very striking figure; as in *Rob Roy* and *Esmond*, it is not to the narrator, but to the people and the events he tells of, that attention is riveted. But Felix Kennaston, while writing this book, lived the strange life of Horvendile in Kennaston's long, happy hours of writing, in stints which steadily became longer and more pleasurable; and insensibly his existence blended, and was absorbed, into the more colorful life of Horvendile. It was as Horvendile that Kennaston wrote, seeming actually at times to remember what he recorded, rather than to invent. . . .

And he called it inspiration. . . .

So the tale flowed on, telling how Count Emmerick planned a notable marriage-feast for his sister La Beale Ettarre and Sir Guiron des Rocques, with vastly different results from those already recorded,—with the results, in fine, which figure in the printed *Men Who Loved Alison*, wherefrom Ettarre has wholly disappeared, and wherein Horvendile keeps his proper place as a more or less convenient device for getting the tale told.

But to Kennaston that first irrational winding-up of affairs, wherein a world's creator was able to wring only contempt and pity from his puppets—since he had not endowed them with any faculties wherewith to comprehend their creator's nature and intent,—was always the tale's real ending. . . .

So it was that the lonely man lived with his dreams, and toiled for the vision's sake contentedly: and we of Lichfield who were most familiar with Felix Kennaston in the flesh knew nothing then of his mental diversions; and, with knowledge, would probably have liked him not a bit the better. For ordinary human beings, with other normal forms of life, turn naturally toward the sun, and are at their best thereunder; but it is the misfortune of dreamers that their peculiar talents find no exercise in daylight. So we regarded Kennaston with the distrust universally accorded people who need to be meddling with ideas in a world which sustains its mental credit comfortably enough with a current coinage of phrases.

And therefore it well may be that I am setting down his story not all in sympathy, for in perfect candor I never, quite, liked Felix Kennaston. His high-pitched voice in talking, to begin with, was irritating: you knew it was not his natural voice, and found it so entirely senseless for him to speak thus. Then, too, the nervous and trivial grin with which he prefaced almost all his infrequent remarks—and the odd little noise, that was nearly a snigger and just missed being a cough, with which he ended them,—was peculiarly uningratiating in a fat and middle-aged person; his weak eyes very rarely met yours full-gaze; and he was continually handling his face or fidgeting with a cigarette or twisting in his chair. When listening to you he usually nibbled at his finger-nails, and when he talked he had a secretive way of looking at them.

Such habits are not wholly incompatible with wisdom or generosity, and the devil's advocate would not advance them against their possessor's canonization; none the less, in everyday life they make against your enjoying a chat with their possessor: and as for Kennaston's undeniable mental gifts, there is no escaping, at times, the gloomy suspicion that fiddling with pens and ink is, after all, no fit employment for a grown man.

Felix Kennaston, to fix the word, was inadequate. His books apart, he was as a human being a failure. Indeed, in some inexpressible fashion, he impressed you as uneasily shirking life. Certainly he seemed since his marriage to have relinquished all conversational obligements to his wife. She had a curious trick of explaining him, before his face,—in a manner which was not unreminiscent of the lecturer in "side-shows" pointing out the peculiarities of the living skeleton or the glass-eater; but it was done with such ill-concealed pride in him that I found it touching, even when she was boring me about the varieties of food he could not be induced to touch or his finicky passion for saving every bit of string he came across.

That suggests a minor mystery: many women had been fond of Felix Kennaston; and I have yet to find a man who liked him even moderately, to offset the host who marveled, with unseemly epithets, as to what these women saw in him. My wife explains it, rather enigmatically, that he was "just a twoser"; and that, in addition, he expected women to look after him, so that naturally they did. To her superior knowledge of the feminine mind I can but bow: with the addition (quoting the same authority) that a "twoser" is a trousered person over-addicted to dumbness in company and to the very thrilliest sort of play-acting in tête-à-têtes.

At all events, I never quite liked Felix Kennaston—not even after I came to understand that the man I knew in the flesh was but a very ill-drawn likeness of Felix Kennaston. After all, that is the whole sardonic point of his story,—and, indeed, of every human story,—that the person you or I find in the mirror is condemned eternally to misrepresent us in the eyes of our fellows. But even with comprehension, I never cordially liked the man; and so it may well be that hereinafter his story is set down not all in sympathy.

With which Gargantuan parenthesis, in equitable warning, I return again to his story.

CHAPTER **10**

Of Idle Speculations in a Library

FELIX KENNASTON did not write very long that night. He fell idly to the droll familiar wondering how this dull fellow seated here in this luxurious room could actually be Felix Kennaston. . . .

He was glad this spacious and subduedly-glowing place, and all the comfortable appointments of Alcluid, belonged to him. He had seen enough of the scrambling hand-to-mouth makeshifts of poverty, in poverty's heart-depressing habitations, during the thirty-eight years that he weathered through before the simultaneous deaths, through a motor accident, of a semi-mythical personage known since childhood as "your Uncle Henry in Lichfield," and of Uncle Henry's only son as well, had raised Felix Kennaston beyond monetary frets. As yet Kennaston did not very profoundly believe in this unlooked-for turn; and in the library of his fine house in particular he had still a sense of treading alien territory under sufferance.

Yet it was a territory which tempted exploration with alluring vistas. Kennaston had always been, when there was time for it, "very fond of reading," as his wife was used to state in tones of blended patronage and apology. Kathleen Kennaston, in the old days of poverty, had declaimed too many pilfered dicta concerning literary matters to retain any liking for them.

As possibly you may recall, for some years after the death of her first husband, Kathleen Eppes Saumarez had earned precarious bread and butter as a lecturer before women's clubs, and was more or less engaged in journalism, chiefly as a reviewer of current literature. For all books she had thus acquired an abiding dislike. In particular, I think, she loathed the two volumes of "woodland tales" collected in those necessitous years, from her Woman's Page in the *Lichfield Courier-Herald,* for the fickle general reading-public, which then used to follow the life-histories of Bazoo the Bear and Mooshwa the Mink, and other "citizens of the wild," with that incalculable unanimity which to-day may be reserved for the biographies of optimistic orphans, and to-morrow veers to *vies intimes* of high-minded courtesans with hearts of gold. . . . In fine, through a variety of reasons, Mrs. Kennaston quite frankly cared even less for books, as manifestations of art, than does the average tolerably honest woman to whom books do not represent a source of income.

And you may or may not remember, likewise, what Kennaston wrote, about this time, in the "Colophon" to *Men Who Loved Alison.* With increased knowledge of the author, some sentences therein, to me at least, took on larger significance:

"No one, I take it, can afford to do without books unless he be quite sure that his own day and personality are the best imaginable; and for this class of persons the most crying need is not, of course, seclusion in a library, but in a sanatorium.

"It was, instead, for the great generality, who combine a taste for travel with a dislike for leaving home, that books were by the luckiest hit invented, to confound the restrictions of geography and the almanac. In consequence, from the Ptolemies to the Capets, from the twilight of a spring dawn in Sicily to the uglier shadow of Montfaucon's gibbet, there intervenes but the turning of a page, a choice between Theocritus and Villon. From the Athens of

Herodotus to the Versailles of Saint-Simon, from Naishapur to Cranford, it is equally quick traveling. All times and lands that ever took the sun, indeed, lie open, equally, to the explorer by the grace of Gutenberg; and transportation into Greece or Rome or Persia or Chicago, equally, is the affair of a moment. Then, too, the islands of Avalon and Ogygia and Theleme stay always accessible, and magic casements open readily upon the surf of Sea-coast Bohemia. For the armchair traveler alone enjoys enfranchisement of a chronology, and of a geography, that has escaped the wear-and-tear of ever actually existing.

"Peregrination in the realms of gold possesses also the quite inestimable advantage that therein one's personality is contraband. As when Dante makes us free of Hell and Heaven, it is on the fixed condition of our actual love and hate of divers Renaissance Italians, whose exploits in the flesh require to-day the curt elucidation of a footnote, just so, admission to those high delights whereunto Shelley conducts is purchased by accrediting to clouds and skylarks—let us sanely admit,—a temporary importance which we would never accord them unbiased. The traveler has for the half-hour exchanged his personality for that of his guide: such is the rule in literary highways, a very necessary traffic ordinance: and so long as many of us are, upon the whole, inferior to Dante or Shelley,—or Sophocles, or Thackeray, or even Shakespeare,—the change need not make entirely for loss. . . ."

Yes, it is lightly phrased; but, after all, it is only another way of confessing that his books afforded Kennaston an avenue to forgetfulness of that fat pasty fellow whom Kennaston was heartily tired of being. For one, I find the admission significant of much, in view of what befell him afterward.

And besides,—so Kennaston's thoughts strayed at times,—these massed books, which his predecessor at Alcluid had acquired piecemeal through the term of a long life, were a part of that predecessor's personality. No other man would have gathered and have preserved precisely the same books, and each book, with varying forcefulness, had entered into his predecessor's mind and had tinged it. These parti-colored books, could one but reconstruct the mosaic correctly, would give a candid portrait of "your Uncle Henry in Lichfield," which would perhaps surprise all those who had known old Henry Kennaston daily in the flesh. Of the fact that these were unusual books their present owner and tentative explorer had no doubt whatever. They were perturbing books.

Now these books by their pleasant display of gold-leaf, soberly aglow in lamplight, recalled an obscure association of other tiny brilliancies; and Felix Kennaston recollected the bit of metal he had found that evening.

Laid by the lamp, it shone agreeably as Kennaston puckered his protruding brows over the characters with which it was inscribed. So far as touched his chances of deciphering them, he knew all foreign languages were to him of almost equal inscrutability. French he could puzzle out, or even Latin, if you gave him plenty of time and a dictionary; but this inscription was not in Roman lettering. He wished, with time-dulled yearning, that he had been accorded a college education. . . .

CHAPTER 11

How There Was a
Light in the Fog

AS SHE CAME toward him through the fog, "How annoying it is," she was saying plaintively, "that these moors are never properly lighted."

"Ah, but you must not blame Ole-Luk-Oie," he protested, "It is all the fault of Beatricê Cenci. . . ."

Then Kennaston knew he had unwittingly spoken magic words, for at once, just as he had seen it done in theaters, the girl's face was shown him clearly in a patch of roseate light. It was the face of Ettarre.

"Things happen so in dreams," he observed. "I know

perfectly well I am dreaming, as I have very often known before this that I was dreaming. But it was always against some law to tell the people in my nightmares that I quite understood they were not real people. To-day in my daydream, and here again to-night, there is no such restriction; and lovely as you are, I know that you are just a daughter of subconsciousness or of memory or of jumpy nerves or, perhaps, of an improperly digested entrée."

"No, I am real, Horvendile,—but it is I who am dreaming you."

"I had not thought to be a part of any woman's dream nowadays. . . . Why do you call me Horvendile?"

She who bore the face of Ettarre pondered momentarily; and his heart moved with glad adoration.

"Now, by the beard of the prophet! I do not know," the girl said, at last.

"The name means nothing to you?"

Ettarre replied pensively: "I never heard that name before. But it seemed natural, somehow,—just as it did when you spoke of Ole-Luk-Oie and Beatricê Cenci."

"But Ole-Luk-Oie is the lord and master of all dreams," said Kennaston. "And that furtive long-dead Roman girl has very often troubled my dreams. . . . When I was a boy, you conceive, there was in my room, at the first boarding-house in which I can remember dieting, a copy of the Guido portrait of Beatricê Cenci,—a copy done in oils, a worthless daub, I suppose. But there was evil in the picture,—a lurking devilishness, which waited, patiently and alertly, until I should do what that silent watcher knew I was predestined to do, and, being malevolent, wanted me to do. I knew nothing then of Beatricê Cenci, mark you, but when I came to learn her history I thought the world was all wrong about her. That woman was evil, whatever verse-makers may have fabled, I thought for a long while. . . . To-day I believe the evil emanated from the person who painted that particular copy. I do not know who that person was, I never shall know. But the black magic of that person's work was very potent."

And Kennaston looked about him now, to find fog everywhere,—impenetrable vapors which vaguely showed pearl-colored radiancies here and there, but no determina-

ble forms of trees or of houses, or of anything save the face
of Ettarre, so clearly discerned and so lovely in that strange
separate cloud of roseate light.

"Ah, yes, those little magics,"—it was the girl who
spoke,—"those futile troubling necromancies that are
wrought by portraits and unfamiliar rooms and mirrors and
all time-worn glittering objects,—by running waters and the
wind's persistency, and by lonely summer noons in forests.
. . . These are the little magics, that have no large power,
but how inconsequently do they fret upon men's heart-
strings!"

"As if some very feeble force—say, a maimed elf,—were
trying to attract your attention? Yes, I think I understand. It
is droll."

"And how droll, too, it is," the girl marveled, "how
quickly we communicate our thoughts,—even though, if you
notice, you are not really speaking, because your lips are
not moving at all."

"No, they never do in dreams. One never seems, in fact,
to use one's mouth,—you never actually eat anything, you
may also notice, in dreams, even though food is very often
at hand. I suppose it is because all dream food is akin to the
pomegranates of Persephone, so that if you taste it you
cannot ever return again to the workaday world. . . . But
why, I wonder, are we having the same dream?—it rather
savors of Morphean parsimony, don't you think, thus to
make one nightmare serve for two people? Or perhaps it is
the bit of metal I found this afternoon—"

And the girl nodded. "Yes, it is on account of the sigil of
Scoteia. I have the other half, you know."

"What does this mean, Ettarre—?" he began; and reach-
ing forward, was about to touch her, when the universe
seemed to fold about him, just as a hand closes. . . .

And Felix Kennaston was sitting at the writing-table in
the library, with a gleaming scrap of metal before him; and
the clock showed bedtime.

"Well, it is undoubtedly quaint how dreams draw
sustenance from half-forgotten happenings," he reflected.
"To think of my recollecting that weird daub which used to
deface my room in Fairhaven! I had forgotten Beatricê
entirely. And I certainly never spoke of her to any human

being, except of course to Muriel Allardyce. . . . But I would not be at all surprised if I had involuntarily hypnotized myself, sitting here staring at this shiny piece of lead,—you read of such cases. I believe I will put it away, to play with again sometime."

CHAPTER **12**

Of Publishing:
With an Unlikely Appendix

SO KENNASTON preserved this bit of metal. "No fool like an old fool," his common-sense testily assured him. But Felix Kennaston's life was rather barren of interests nowadays. . . .

He thought no more of his queer dream, for a long while. Life had gone on decorously. He had completed *The Audit at Storisende*, with leisured joy in the task, striving to write perfectly of beautiful happenings such as life did not afford. There is no denying that the typed manuscript seemed to Felix Kennaston—as he added the last touches, before expressing it to Dapley & Pildriff,—to inaugurate a new era in literature.

Kennaston was yet to learn that publishers in their business capacity have no especial concern with literature. To his bewilderment he discovered that publishers seemed sure the merits of a book had nothing to do with the advisability of printing it. Herewith is appended a specimen or two from Felix Kennaston's correspondence.

Dapley & Pildriff—"We have carefully read your story, 'The Audit at Storisende,' which you kindly submitted to us. It is needless for us to speak of the literary quality of the story: it is in fact exquisitely done, and would delight a very limited circle of readers trained to appreciate such delicate productions. But that class of readers is necessarily small, and the general reader would, we fear, fail to recognize the book's merit and be attracted to it. For this reason we do not feel—and we regret to confess it,—that the publication of this book would be a wise business enterprise for us to undertake. We wish that we could, in justice to you and ourselves, see the matter in another light. We are returning the manuscript to you, and we remain, with appreciation of your courtesy, etc."

Paige Ticknor's Sons—"We have given very careful consideration to your story, 'The Audit at Storisende,' which you kindly submitted to us. We were much interested in this romance, for it goes without saying that it is marked with high literary quality. But we feel that it would not appeal with force and success to the general reader. Its appeal, we think, would be to the small class of cultured readers, and therefore its publication would not be attended with commercial success. Therefore in your interest, as well as our own, we feel that we must give an unfavorable decision upon the question of publication. Naturally we regret to be forced to that conclusion, for the work is one which would be creditable to any publisher's list. We return the manuscript by express, with our appreciation of your courtesy in giving us the opportunity of considering it, and are, etc."

And so it was with the Gayvery Company, and with Leeds, McKibble & Todd, and with Stuyvesant & Brothers. Unanimously they united to praise and to return the manuscript. And Kennaston began reluctantly to suspect that, for all their polite phrases about literary excellence, his romance must, somehow, be not quite in consonance with the standards of that person who is, after all, the final arbiter of literature, and to whom these publishers very properly deferred, as "the general reader." And Kennaston wondered if it would not be well for him, also, to study the all-important and exigent requirements of "the general reader."

Kennaston turned to the publishers' advertisements. Dapley & Pildriff at that time were urging everyone to read *White Sepulchers*, the author of which had made public the momentous discovery that all churchgoers were not immaculate persons. Paige Ticknor's Sons were announcing a "revised version" of *The Apostates,*—by Kennaston's own loathed first-cousin,—which was guaranteed to sear the soul to its core, more than rival Thackeray, and turn our highest social circles inside out. Then the Gayvery Company offered *Through the Transom*, a daring study of "feminism," compiled to all appearance under rather novel conditions, inasmuch as the brilliant young author had, according to the advertisements, written every sentence with his jaws set and his soul on fire. The majority of Leeds, McKibble & Todd's adjectives were devoted to *Sarah's Secret*, the prize-winner in the firm's $15,000 contest,—a "sprightly romance of the greenwood," whose undoubted aim, Kennaston deduced from tentative dips into its meandering balderdash, was to become the most-sought-after book in all institutes devoted to care of the feeble-minded. And Stuyvesant & Brothers were superlatively acclaiming *The Silent Brotherhood*, the latest masterpiece of a pornographically gifted genius, who had edifyingly shown that he ranked religion above literature, by retiring from the ministry to write novels.

Kennaston laughed,—upon which side of the mouth, it were too curious to inquire. Momentarily he thought of printing the book at his own expense. But here the years of poverty had left indelible traces. Kennaston had too often walked because he had not carfare, for a dollar ever again to seem to him an inconsiderable matter. Comfortably reassured as to pecuniary needs for the future, he had not the least desire to control more money than actually showed in his bank-balances: but, even so, he often smiled to note how unwillingly he spent money. So now he shrugged, and sent out his loved romance again.

An unlikely thing happened: the book was accepted for publication. The Baxon-Muir Company had no prodigious faith in *The Audit at Storisende*, as a commercial venture; but their "readers," in common with most of the "readers" for the firms who had rejected it, were not lacking in discernment of its merits as an admirable piece of writing. And the more optimistic among them protested even to foresee a possibility of the book's selling. The vast public that reads for pastime, they contended, was beginning to grow a little tired of being told how bad was this or that economic condition: and pretty much everything had been "daringly exposed," to the point of weariness, from the inconsistencies of our clergy to the uncleanliness of our sausage. In addition, they considered the surprising success of Mr. Marmaduke Fennel's eighteenth-century story, *For Love of a Lady*, as compared with the more moderate sales of Miss Elspeth Lancaster's *In Scarlet Sidon*, that candid romance of the brothel; deducing therefrom that the "gadzooks" and "by'r lady" type of reading-matter was ready to revive in vogue. At all events, the Baxon-Muir Company, after holding a rather unusual number of conferences, declared their willingness to publish this book; and in due course they did publish it.

There were before this, however, for Kennaston many glad hours of dabbling with proof-sheets: the tale seemed so different, and so infernally good, in print. Kennaston never in his life found any other playthings comparable to those first wide-margined "galley proofs" of *The Audit at Storisende.* Here was the word, vexatiously repeated within three lines, which must be replaced by a synonym; and the clause which, when transposed, made the whole sentence gain in force and comeliness; and the curt sentence whose addition gave clarity to the paragraph, much as a pinch of alum clears turbid water; and the vaguely unsatisfactory adjective, for which a jet of inspiration suggested a substitute, of vastly different meaning, in the light of whose inevitable aptness you marveled over your preliminary obtuseness:—all these slight triumphs, one by one, first gladdened Kennaston's labor and tickled his self-complacency. He could see no fault in the book.

His publishers had clearer eyes. His preface, for one matter, they insisted on transposing to the rear of the volume, where it now figures as the book's tolerably famous Colophon,—that curious exposition of Kennaston's creed as artist. Then, for a title, *The Audit at Storisende* was editorially adjudged abominable: people would not know how to pronounce Storisende, and in consequence would hold back from discussing the romance or even asking for it at book-dealers. *Men Who Loved Ettarre* was Kennaston's ensuing suggestion; but the Baxon-Muir Company showed

no fixed confidence in their patrons' ability to pronounce
Ettarre, either. Would it not be possible, they inquired, to
change the heroine's name?—and Kennaston assented. Thus
it was that in the end his book came to be called *Men Who
Loved Alison.*

But to Kennaston her name stayed always Ettarre. . . .

The book was delivered to the world, which received the
gift without excitement. The book was delivered to
reviewers, who found in it a well-intentioned echo of Mr.
Maurice Hewlett's earlier mediaeval tales. And there, for a
month or some six weeks, the matter rested.

Then, one propitious morning, an indignant gentlewoman
in Brooklyn wrote to *The New York Sphere* a letter which
was duly printed in that journal's widely circulated Sunday
supplement, *The Literary Masterpieces of This Week,* to
denounce the loathsome and depraved indecency of the
nineteenth and twentieth chapters, in which—while treating
of Sir Guiron's imprisonment in the Sacred Grove of Caer
Idryn, and the worship accorded there to the sigil of
Scoteia,—Kennaston had touched upon some of the perverse
refinements of antique sexual relations. The following week
brought forth a full page of letters. Two of these, as
Kennaston afterward learned, were contributed by the
"publicity man" of the Baxon-Muir Company, and all
arraigned obscenities which Kennaston could neither remember nor on re-reading his book discover. Later in this
journal, as in other newspapers, appeared still more
denunciations. An up-to-the-minute bishop expostulated
from the pulpit against the story's vicious tendencies,
demanding that it be suppressed.

Thereafter it was no longer on sale in the large
department-stores alone, but was equally procurable at all
the bookstands in hotels and railway stations. Even the
author's acquaintances began to read it. And the Delaunays
(then at the height of their vogue as exponents of the "new"
dances) introduced "the Alison amble"; and from Tampa to
Seattle, in certain syndicated cartoons of generally appeal-
ing idiocy, newspaper readers were privileged to see one
hero of the series knock the other heels over head with a
copy of Kennaston's romance. And women wore the "Alison
aigrette" for a whole season; and a new brand of cheap

tobacco christened in her honor had presently made her
name at least familiar in saloons. *Men Who Loved Alison*
became, in fine, the novel of the hour. It was one of those
rare miracles such as sometimes palm off a well-written
book upon the vast public that reads for pastime.

And shortly afterward Mr. Booth Tarkington published
another of his delightful saccharine romances: one forgets at
this distance of time just which it was: but, like all the other
Tarkingtonian tales of the triumph of honest worth in
somewhat melodramatic circumstances, it was exquisitely
done, and sold neck and neck with *Men Who Loved Alison;*
so that for a while it looked almost as if the American
reading public was coming to condone adroit and careful
composition.

But presently the advertising columns of magazines and
newspapers were heralding the year's vernal output of
enduring masterworks in the field of fiction: and readers
were again assured that the great American novel had just
been published at last, by any number of persons: and so,
the autumnal predecessors of these new chefs d'oeuvre
passed swiftly into oblivion, via the brief respite of a
"popular" edition. And naturally, Kennaston's romance was
forgotten, by all save a few pensive people. Some of them
had found in this volume food for curious speculation.

That, however, is a matter to be taken up later.

CHAPTER **13**

Suggesting Themes of
Universal Appeal

SO FELIX KENNASTON saw his dream vulgarized, made
a low byword; and he contemplated this travestying, as the
cream of a sardonic jest, with urbanity. Indeed, that hour of
notoriety seemed not without its pleasant features to Felix

Kennaston, who had all a poet's ordinary appetite for flattery. Besides, it was droll to read the "literary notes" which the Baxon-Muir people were industriously disseminating, by means of the daily journals, as to this Felix Kennaston's personality, ancestry, accomplishments, recreations and preferences in diet. And then, in common with the old woman famed in nursery rhyme, he was very often wont to observe, "But, lawk a mercy on me! this is none of I!"

It was droll, too, to be asked for autographs, lectures, and for donations of "your wonderful novel." It was droll to receive letters from remote mysterious persons, who had read his book, and had liked it, or else had disliked it to the point of being goaded into epistolary remonstrance, sarcasm, abuse, and (as a rule) erratic spelling. And it was droll to be having so many scented letters from strange women whose designs as to his physical chastity were wholly frank. Yet it troubled Kennaston that only riffraff seemed to have read his book, so far as he could judge from these unsolicited communications; and that such people of culture and education as might have been thrilled by it—all people whose opinions he might conceivably value,—seemed never to write to authors. . . .

And finally, it was droll to watch his wife's reception of the book. To Kennaston his wife stayed always a not unfriendly mystery. She now could not but be a little taken aback by this revelation of his abilities, he reflected,—with which she had lived so long without, he felt, appreciation of them,—but he well knew she would never admit either fact. He much doubted if Kathleen would ever actually read *Men Who Loved Alison;* on various pretexts she had deferred the pleasure, and seemed, with perverted notions of humor, to esteem it a joke that she alone had not read the book of which everybody was talking. Such was not Kennaston's idea of humor, or of wifely interest. But Kathleen dipped into the volume here and there; and she assuredly read all the newspaper-notices sent in by the clipping-bureau. These she considered with profound seriousness.

"I have been thinking—you ought to make a great deal out of your next novel," she said, one morning, over her grapefruit.

Then the former poet wondered why, in heaven's name, it

should matter to her whether or not the marketing of his dreams earned money, when he and she had already a competence. But women were thus fashioned. . . .

"You ought to do something more up-to-date, though, Felix, something that deals with real life—"

"Ah, but I don't particularly care to write about a subject of which I am so totally ignorant, dear. Besides, it isn't for you to fleer and gibe at a masterpiece which you have never read," he airily informed her.

"I am saving it up for next summer, Felix, when I shall have a chance to give every word of it the reverence it deserves. I really don't have any time for reading nowadays. There is always something that simply has to be attended to—For instance, the gasoline engine isn't working again, and I had to 'phone in town for Slaytor to send a man out to-day, to see what is the matter this time."

"And it is messy things like that you want me to write about!" he exclaimed. "About the gasoline engine going on another strike, and Drake's forgetting to tell you we were all out of sugar until late Saturday night! Never mind, Mrs. Kennaston! you will be sorry for this, and you will weep the bitter tears of unavailing repentance, some day, when you ride in the front automobile with the Governor to the unveiling of my various monuments, and have fallen into the anecdotage of a great man's widow."

He spoke lightly, but he was reflecting that in reality Kathleen did not read his book because she did not regard any of his doings very seriously.

"Isn't this the third time this week we have had herring for breakfast?" he inquired, pleasantly. "I think I will wait and let them scramble me a couple of eggs. It is evidently a trifle that has escaped your attention, my darling, during our long years of happy married life, that I don't eat herring. But of course, just as you say, you have a number of more important and more practical topics than husbands to think about. I dislike having to put anyone to any extra trouble on my account; but as it happens, I have a lot of work to do this morning, and I cannot very well get through it on an empty stomach."

"We haven't had it since Saturday, Felix." Then Kathleen said, with aloof weariness, to the serving-girl, "Cora, see if

Mr. Kennaston can have some eggs. . . . I do wish, Felix, that you wouldn't upset things so. Your coffee will get stone-cold; and it is hard enough to keep servants as it is. Besides, you know perfectly well to-day is Thursday, and the library has to be thorough-cleaned."

"That means, of course, I am to be turned out-of-doors and forced to waste a whole day somewhere in town. It is quite touching how my creature comforts are catered to in this house!"

And Kathleen began to laugh, ruefully. "You are just a great big baby, Felix. You are sulking and swelling up like a frog, because you think I don't appreciate what a wonderful husband I have and what a wonderful book he has written."

Then Kennaston began to laugh also. He knew that what she said was tolerably true, even to the batrachian simile. So he answered:

"When you insisted on adopting me, dear, you ought to have realized what you were letting yourself in for."

"—And I do think," Kathleen went on, evincing that conviction with which she as a rule repeated other people's remarks, "that you ought to make your next book something that deals with real life. *Men Who Loved Alison* is beautifully written and all that, but, exactly as the *Tucson Pioneer* said, it is really just colorful soapbubbly nonsense."

"Ah, but is it unadulterated nonsense, Kathleen, that somewhere living may be a uniformly noble transaction?" he debated,—"and human passions never be in a poor way to find expression with adequate speech and action?"

Pleased with the phrase, and feeling in a better temper, he began to butter a roll. And Kathleen said,

"I don't know about that; but, in any event, people prefer to read about the life they are familiar with."

"You touch on a disheartening truth," Kennaston admitted. "People never want to be told anything they do not believe already. Yet I quite fail to see why, in books or elsewhere, anyone should wish to be reminded of what human life is actually like. For living is the one art in which mankind has never achieved distinction. It is perhaps an obscure sense of this that makes us think the begetting of mankind an undiscussable subject, and death a sublime and edifying topic."

"Yes—? I daresay," Kathleen assented vaguely. "This herring is really very good, Felix. I think you would like it, if you just had not made up your mind to be stubborn about it—" Then she spoke with new animation: "Felix, Margaret Woods was in Louvet's yesterday morning, having her hair done for a dinner they gave the railroad crowd last night, and of all the faded washed-out-looking people I ever saw—! And I can remember her having that hideous brown dress long before she was married. Of course, it doesn't make any difference to me that she did not see fit to invite us. She was one of your friends, not mine. I was only thinking that, since she always pretended to be so fond of you, it does seem curious the way we are invariably left out."

She returned then to the gasoline engine which was not working, she touched upon the possibility of there again being a dead frog in the well, she mentioned a number of her relatives who had herring for breakfast almost every morning, and she became emphatic as to the quite dreadful batch of persons who had been elected directors of the Woman's Club. And, as each topic arose, Felix Kennaston made one or another elaborately chilly reply, as he sat waiting, with elaborate patience, for his eggs.

So Kennaston did not embroider verbally his theme—of Living Adequately,—as he had felt himself in vein to do could he have found a listener.

"Some day," he ruefully reflected, in the while that Kathleen spoke of the sort of people that were getting into the Woman's Club nowadays, "I shall certainly write a paper upon The Lost Art of Conversing with One's Wife. Its appeal, I think, would be universal."

Then his eggs came. . . .

CHAPTER 14

Peculiar Conduct of a
Personage

SHORTLY AFTERWARD befell a queer incident. Kennaston, passing through a famed city, lunched with a personage who had been pleased to admire *Men Who Loved Alison,* and whose remunerative admiration had been skilfully trumpeted in the public press by Kennaston's publishers.

There were some ten others in the party, and Kennaston found it droll enough to be sitting at table with them. The lean pensive man—with hair falling over his forehead in a neatly-clipped "bang," such as custom restricts to children,—had probably written that morning, in his official capacity, to innumerable potentates. That handsome bluff old naval officer was a national hero: he would rank in history with Perry and John Paul Jones; yet here he sat, within arm's-reach, prosaically complaining of unseasonable weather. That bearded man, rubicund and monstrous as to nose, was perhaps the most powerful, as he was certainly the most wealthy, person inhabiting flesh; and it was rumored, in those Arcadian days, that kingdoms nowhere might presume to go to war without securing the consent of this financier.

And that exquisitely neat fellow, looking like a lad unconvincingly made-up for an octogenarian in amateur theatricals, was the premier of the largest province in the world: his thin-featured neighbor was an aeronaut,—at this period really a *rara avis,*—and went above the clouds to get his livelihood, just as ordinary people went to banks and offices. And chief of all, their multifarious host—the personage, as one may discreetly call him,—had left unattempted scarcely any rôle in the field of human activities: as ranchman, statesman, warrior, historian, editor, explorer, athlete, coiner of phrases, and rediscoverer of the Decalogue, impartially, he had labored to make the world a

livelier place of residence; and already he was the pivot of
as many legends as Charlemagne or Arthur.

The famous naval officer, as has been said, was complaining of the weather. "The seasons have changed so, since I
can remember. We seem to go straight from winter into
summer nowadays."

"It has been rather unseasonable," assented the financier;
"but then you always feel the heat so much more during the
first few hot days."

"Besides," came the judicious comment, "it has not been
the heat which was so oppressive this morning, I think, as
the great amount of humidity in the air."

"Yes, it is most unpleasant,—makes your clothes stick to
you so."

"Ah, but don't you find, now," asked the premier gaily,
"that looking at the thermometer tends to make you feel,
really, much more uncomfortable than if you stayed
uninformed as to precisely how hot it was?"

"Well! where ignorance is bliss it is folly to be wise, as I
remember to have seen stated somewhere."

"By George, though, it is wonderful how true are many of
those old sayings!" observed the personage. "We assume we
are much wiser than our fathers: but I doubt if we really
are, in the big things that count."

"In fact, I have often wondered what George Washington,
for example, would think of the republic he helped to
found, if he could see it nowadays."

"He would probably find it very different from what he
imagined it would be."

"Why, he would probably turn in his grave, at some of our
newfangled notions,—such as prohibition and equal suf-
frage."

"Oh, well, all sensible people know, of course, that the
trouble with prohibition is that it does not prohibit, and that
woman's place is the home, not in the mire of politics."

"That is admirably put, sir, if you will permit me to say
so. Still, there is a great deal to be said on both sides."

"And after all, is there not a greater menace to the ideals
of Washington and Jefferson in the way our present laws
tend uniformly to favor rich people?"

"There you have it, sir,—to-day we punish the poor man

for doing what the rich man does with entire impunity, only
on a larger scale."

"By George, there are many of our so-called captains of
industry who, if the truth were told, and a shorter and uglier
word were not unpermissible, are little better than malefac-
tors of great wealth."

This epigram, howsoever heartily admired, was felt by
many of the company to be a bit daring in the presence of
the magnate: and the lean Secretary of State spoke hastily,
or at any rate, in less leisurely tones than usual, now that he
pointed out:

"After all, money is not everything. The richest people
are not always the happiest, in spite of their luxury."

"You gentlemen can take it from me," asserted the
aeronaut, "that many poor people get a lot of pleasure out of
life."

"Now, really though, that reminds me—children are very
close observers, and, as you may have noticed, they ask the
most remarkable questions. My little boy asked me, only
last Tuesday, why poor people are always so polite and
kind—"

"Well, little pitchers have big ears—"

"What you might call a chip of the old block, eh?—so
that mighty little misses him?"

"I may be prejudiced, but I thought it pretty good,
coming from a kid of six—"

"And it is perfectly true, gentlemen,—the poor are kind to
each other. Now, I believe just being kind makes you
happier—"

"And I often think that is a better sort of religion than just
dressing up in your best clothes and going to church
regularly on Sundays—"

"That is a very true thought," another chimed in.

"And expressed, upon my word, with admirable clarity—"

"Oh, whatever pretended pessimists in search of notoriety
may say, most people are naturally kind, at heart—"

"I would put it that Christianity, in spite of the carping
sneers of science so-called, has led us once for all to
recognize the vast brotherhood of man—"

"So that, really, the world gets better every day—"

"We have quite abolished war, for instance—"

"My dear sir, were there nothing else, and even putting aside the outraged sentiments of civilized humanity, another great or prolonged war between any two of the leading nations is unthinkable—"

"For the simple reason, gentlemen, that we have perfected our fighting machines to such an extent that the destruction involved would be too frightful—"

"Then, too, we are improving the automobile to such an extent—"

"Oh, in the end it will inevitably supplant the horse—"

"It seems almost impossible to realize how we ever got along without the automobile—"

"Do you know, I would not be surprised if some day horses were exhibited in museums—"

"As rare and nearly extinct animals? Come, now, that is pretty good—"

"And electricity is, as one might say, just in its infancy—"

"The telephone, for instance,—our ancestors would not have believed in the possibilities of such a thing—"

"And, by George, they talk of giving an entire play with those moving-picture machines,—acting the whole thing out, you know."

"Oh, yes, we live in the biggest, brainiest age the world has ever known—"

"And America is going to be the greatest nation in it, before very long, commercially and in every way. . . ."

So the talk flowed on, with Felix Kennaston contributing very little thereto. Indeed, Felix Kennaston, the dreamer, was rather ill-at-ease among these men of action, and listened to their observations with perturbed attention. He sat among the great ones of earth,—not all of them the very greatest, of course, but each a person of quite respectable importance. It was the sort of gathering that in boyhood—and in later life also, for that matter,—he had foreplanned to thrill and dazzle, as he perfectly recollected. But now, with the opportunity, he somehow could not think of anything quite suitable to say,—of anything which would at once do him justice and be admiringly received.

Therefore he attempted to even matters by assuring himself that the talk of these efficient people was lacking in brilliance and real depth, and expressed sentiments which, microscopically viewed, did not appear to be astoundingly original. If these had been less remarkable persons he would have thought their conversation almost platitudinous. And not one of them, howsoever distinguished, or whatsoever else he might have done, could have written *Men Who Loved Alison!* Kennaston cherished that reflection as he sedately partook of a dish he recollected to have seen described, on menu cards, as "Hungarian goulash" and sipped sherry of no very extraordinary flavor. . . .

He was to remember how plain the fare was, and more than once, was to refer to this meal—quite casually,— through a "That reminds me of what Such-an-one said once, when I was lunching with him," or perhaps, "The last time I lunched with So-and-so, I remember—" With such gambits he was to begin, later, to introduce to us of Lichfield divers anecdotes which, if rather pointless, were at least garnished with widely-known names.

There was a Cabinet meeting that afternoon, and, luncheon ended, the personage wasted scant time in dismissing his guests.

"It has been a very great pleasure to meet you, Mr. Kennaston," quoth the personage, wringing Kennaston's hand.

Kennaston suitably gave him to understand that they shared ecstasy in common. But all the while Kennaston was, really, thinking that here before him, half-revealed, shone the world-famous teeth portrayed by cartoonists in the morning-paper every day, everywhere. Yes, they were remarkable teeth,—immaculate, marmoreal and massive, —and they were so close-set that Kennaston was now smitten with an idiotic desire to ask their owner if the personage could get dental floss between them. . . .

"Those portions of your book relating to the sigil of Scoteia struck me as being too explicit," the personage continued, bluffly, but in lowered tones. The two stood now, beneath a great stuffed elk's head, a little apart from the others. "Do you think it was quite wise? I seem to recall a phrase—about birds—"

Kennaston's thoughts remained, as yet, dental. But there is no denying Kennaston was perturbed. Nor was he less puzzled when, as if in answer to Kennaston's bewildered look, the personage produced from his waistcoat pocket a small square mirror, which he half-exhibited, but retained secretively in the palm of his hand. "Yes, the hurt may well be two-fold—I am pre-supposing that, as a country gentleman, you have raised white pigeons, Mr. Kennaston?" he said, meaningly.

"Why, no, they keep up such a maddening cooing and purring on warm days, and drum so on tin roofs"—Kennaston stammered,—"that I long ago lost patience with the birds of Venus, whatever the tincture of their plumage. There used to be any number of them on our place, though—"

"Ah, well," the personage said, with a wise nod, and with more teeth than ever, "you exercise a privilege common to all of us,—and my intended analogy falls through. In any event, it has been a great pleasure to meet you. Come and see me again, Mr. Kennaston,—and meanwhile, think over what I have said."

And that was all. Kennaston returned to Alcluid in a whirl of formless speculations. The mirror and the insane query as to white pigeons could not, he considered, but constitute some password to which Kennaston had failed to give the proper response.

The mystery had some connection with what he had written in his book as to the sigil of Scoteia. . . . And he could not find he had written anything very definite. The broken disk was spoken of as a talisman in the vague terms best suited to a discussion of talismans by a person who knew nothing much about them. True, the book told what the talisman looked like; it looked like that bit of metal he had picked up in the garden. . . . He wondered if he had thrown away that bit of metal; and, searching, discovered it in the desk drawer, where it had lain for several months.

Laid by the lamp, it shone agreeably as Kennaston puckered his protruding heavy brows over the characters with which it was inscribed. That was what the sigil looked like,—or, rather, what half the sigil looked like, because Ettarre still had the other half. How could the personage have known anything about it? unless there were, indeed, really some secret and some password through which men won to place and the world's prizes? . . . Blurred memories of Eugene Sue's nefarious Jesuits and of Balzac's redoubtable Thirteen arose in the background of his mental picturings. . . .

No, the personage had probably been tasting beverages more potent than sherry; there were wild legends, since disproved, such as seemed then to excuse that supposition: or perhaps he was insane, and nobody but Felix Kennaston knew it. . . . What could a little mirror, or, of all things, pigeons, have to do with this bit of metal?—except that this bit of metal, too, reflected light so that the strain tired your eyes, thus steadily to look down upon this timeworn glittering object. . . .

CHAPTER **15**

Of Vain Regret and Wonder in the Dark

MADAM," he was insanely stating, "I would not for the world set up as a fit exponent for the mottoes of a copybook: but I am not all base."

"You are," flashed she, "a notorious rogue."

It was quite dark. Kennaston could not see the woman with whom he was talking. But they were in an open paved place, like a courtyard, and he was facing the great shut door against which she stood, vaguely discernible. He knew they were waiting for someone to open this door. It seemed to him, for no reason at all, that they were at Tunbridge Wells.

But there was no light anywhere. Complete darkness submerged them; the skies showed not one glimmer. And he was replying:

"That I am of smirched repute, madam, I lack both grounds and inclination to deny. Yet I am not so through choice. Believe me, I am innately a lover of all bodily comforts: so, by preference, an ill name is as obnoxious to me as—shall we say?—soiled linen or a coat of last year's cut. But then, *que voulez-vous?* as our lively neighbors observe. Squeamishness was never yet bred in an empty pocket; and I am thus compelled to the commission of divers profitable peccadillos, once in a blue moon, by the dictates of that same haphazard chance which to-night has pressed me into the service of innocence and virtue."

She kept silence; and he went on in lightheaded wonder as to what this dream, so plainly recognized as such, was all about, and as to whence came the words which sprang so nimbly to his lips, and as to what was the cause of his great wistful sorrow. Perhaps if he listened very attentively to what he was saying, he might find out. He noticed that he was saying now:

"You do not answer, madam. Yet think a little. I am a notorious rogue: the circumstance is conceded. But do you think I have selfishly become so in quest of amusement? Nay, I can assure you that Newgate, the wigged judge, the jolting cart, the gallows, blend in no pleasant dreams. . . . But what choice had I? Cast forth to the gutter's miring in the susceptible years of infancy, a girl of the town's byblow, what choice had I, in heaven's name? If I may not live as I would, I must live as I may; in emperors and parsons and sewer-diggers and cheese-mites that claim is equally allowed."

"You are a thief?" she asked, pensively.

"Let us put it, rather, that I have proved in life's hard school an indifferent Latinist, by occasionally confounding *tuum* with *meum*."

"A murderer?"

"Something of the sort might be my description in puritanic mouths. You know at least what happened at The Cat and Hautbois."

("*But what in the world had happened there?*" Kennaston wondered.)

"And yet—" The sweet voice marveled.

"And yet I have saved you from Lord Umfraville? Ah, madam, Providence labors with quaint instruments, dilapidating Troy by means of a wood rocking-horse, and loosing sin into the universe through a half-eaten apple.

Nay, I repeat, I am not all base; and I have read somewhere that those who are in honor wholly shipwrecked will yet very often cling desperately to one stray spar of virtue."

He could tell her hand had raised to the knocker on the closed door. "Mr. Vanringham, will you answer me a question?"

"A thousand. *(So I am Vanringham.)*"

The girl continued: "I have not knocked. I possess, as you know, a considerable fortune in my own right. It would be easy for a strong man—and, sure, your shoulders are prodigiously broad, Mr. Cutthroat!—very easy for him to stifle my cries and carry me away, even now. And then, to preserve my honor, I would have no choice save to marry that broad-shouldered man. Is this not truth?"

"It is the goddess herself, newly stolen from her well. *O dea certé!*"

"I am not absolutely hideous, either?" she queried, absent-mindedly.

"Dame Venus," Kennaston observed, "may have made a similar demand of the waves at Cythera when she first rose among their billows: and I doubt not that the white foaming waters, amorously clutching at her far whiter feet, laughed and murmured the answer I would give did I not know your question was put in a spirit of mockery."

"And yet—" she re-began.

"And yet," the man echoed, "yet I resist all these temptations? Frankly, had you been in my eyes less desirable, madam, you would not have reached home thus uneventfully; for a rich marriage is the only chance adapted to repair my tattered fortunes; and the devil is cunning to avail himself of our flesh's frailty. Had you been the fat widow of some City knight I would have played my lord of Umfraville's part, upon my pettier scale. Or, had I esteemed it possible for me to have done with my old life, I would have essayed to devote a cleaner existence to your service and worship. Indeed, indeed, I speak the truth, howsoever jestingly!" he said, with sudden wildness. "But what would you have? I would not entrust your fan, much less your happiness, to the keeping of a creature so untrustworthy as I know myself to be. In fine, I look upon you, madam, in such rapture of veneration and tenderness and joy and heartbreaking yearning, that it is necessary I get very tipsy to-night, and strive to forget that I, too, might have lived cleanlily."

And Kennaston, as he spoke thus, engulfed in darkness, knew it was a noble sorrow which possessed him,—a stingless wistful sorrow such as is aroused by the unfolding of a well-acted tragedy or the progress of a lofty music. This ruffian longing, quite hopelessly, to be made clean again, so worshipful of his loved lady's purity and loveliness, and knowing loveliness and purity to be forever unattainable in his mean life, was Felix Kennaston, somehow. . . . What was it Maugis d'Aigremont had said?—"I have been guilty of many wickednesses, I have held much filthy traffic such as my soul loathed; and yet, I swear to you, I seem to myself to be still the boy who once was I." Kennaston understood now, for the first time with deep reality, what his puppet had meant; and how a man's deeds in the flesh may travesty the man himself.

But the door opened. Confusedly Kennaston was aware of brilliantly-lighted rooms beyond, of the chatter of gay people, of thin tinkling music, and, more immediately, of two lackeys, much bepowdered as to their heads, and stately in new liveries of blue-and-silver. Confusedly he noted these things, for the woman had paused in the bright doorway, and all the loveliness of Ettarre was visible now, and she had given a delighted cry of recognition.

"La, it is Horvendile! and we are having the same dream again!"

This much he heard and saw as her hand went out toward him gladly. Then as she touched him the universe seemed to fold about Felix Kennaston, just as a hand closes, and he was sitting at the writing-table in the library, with a gleaming scrap of metal before him.

He sat thus for a long while.

"I can make nothing of all this. I remember of course that I saw Muriel Allardyce stand very much like that, in the doorway of the Royal Hotel, at the Green Chalybeate,—and how many years ago, good Lord! . . . And equally of course the most plausible explanation is that I am losing my wits. Or, else, it may be that I am playing blindfold with perilous matters. Felix Kennaston, my friend, the safest plan—the one assuredly safe plan for you,—would be to throw away this devil's toy, and forget it completely. . . . And, I will, too,—the very first thing to-morrow morning,— or after I have had a few days to think it over, any way. . . ."

But even as he made this compact it was without much lively faith in his promises.

PART THREE

**Which points the truism that
many more lead double lives
than confess to it**

*"Come to me in my dreams, and then
By day I shall be well again!
For then the night will more than pay
The hopeless longing of long day.*

*"Come, as thou cam'st a thousand times,
A messenger from lovelier climes,
To smile on our drear world, and be
As king to others as to me!"*

CHAPTER 16

They Come to a High Place

HE WAS LOOKING down at the most repulsive old woman he had ever seen. Hers was the abhorrent fatness of a spider; her flesh appeared to have the coloring and consistency of dough. She sat upon the stone pavement, knitting; her eyes, which raised to his unblinkingly, were black, secretive, and impersonally malevolent; and her jaws stirred without ceasing, in a loose chewing motion, so that the white hairs, rooted in the big mole on her chin, twitched and glittered in the sunlight.

"But one does not pay on entering," she was saying. "One pays as one goes out. It is the rule."

"And what do you knit, mother?" he asked.

"Eh, I shall never know until God's funeral is preached," the old woman said. "I only know it is forbidden me to stop."

So he went past her, aware that, through some nameless grace, the girl whom he had twice seen in dreams awaited him there, and that the girl's face was the face of Ettarre. She stood by a stone balustrade, upon which squatted tall stone monsters,—weird and haphazard collocations, as touched anatomy, of bird and brute and fiend,—and she in common with these hobgoblins looked down upon a widespread comely city. The time was a bright and windy morning in spring; and the sky, unclouded, was like an inverted cup which did not merely roof Ettarre and the man who had come back to her, but inclosed them in incommunicable isolation. To the left, beyond shimmering tree-tops, so far beneath them that it made Felix Kennaston dizzy to look, the ruffling surface of a river gleamed. . . . It was in much this fashion, he recalled, that Ettarre and

87

Horvendile had stood alone together among the turrets of Storisende.

"But now I wonder where on the face of—or, rather, so far above the face of what especial planet we may happen to be?" Kennaston marveled happily,—"or east of the sun or west of the moon? At all events, it hardly matters. Suffice it that we are in love's land to-day. What need is there to worry over any one inexplicable detail, where everything is incomprehensible?"

"I was never here before, Horvendile; and I have waited for you so long."

He looked at her; and again his heart moved with glad adoration. It was not merely that Ettarre was so pleasing to the eye, and distinguished by so many delicate clarities of color,—so young, so quick of movement, so slender, so shapely, so inexpressibly virginal,—but the heady knowledge that here on dizzying heights he, Felix Kennaston, was somehow playing with superhuman matters, and that no power could induce him to desist from his delicious and perilous frolic, stirred, in deep recesses of his being, nameless springs. Nameless they must remain; for it was as though he had discovered himself to possess a sixth sense; and he found that the contrivers of language, being less prodigally gifted, had never been at need to invent any terms wherewith to express this sense's gratification. But he knew that he was strong and admirable; that men and men's affairs lay far beneath him; that Ettarre belonged to him; and that the exultance which now possessed him was the by-product of an unstable dream.

"Yet it is not any city of to-day," he was saying. "Look how yonder little rascal glitters,—he is wearing a helmet of some sort and a gorget. Why, all those pigmies, if you look closely, go in far braver scarlets and purples that we elect to skulk about in nowadays; and nowhere in sight is an office-building or an electric-light advertisement of chewing-gum. No, that hotchpotch of huddled gables and parapets and towers shaped like lanterns was stolen straight out of some Doré illustration for Rabelais or *Les Contes Drolatiques*. But it does not matter at all, and it will never matter, Ettarre, where we may chance to be. What really

and greatly matters, is that when I try to touch you everything vanishes."

The girl was frankly puzzled. "Yes, that seems a part of the
sigil's magic. . . ."

CHAPTER 17

Of the Sigil and
One Use of It

IT PROVED THAT this was indeed a part of the sigil's
wonder-working: Kennaston learned by experience that
whenever, even by accident, he was about to touch Ettarre
his dream would end like a burst bubble. He would find
himself alone and staring at the gleaming fragment of metal.

Before long he also learned something concerning the
sigil of Scoteia, of which this piece of metal once formed a
part; for it was permitted him to see the sigil in its entirety,
many centuries before it was shattered: it was then one of
the treasures of the Didascalion, a peculiar sort of girl's
school in King Ptolemy Physcon's city of Alexandria, where
women were tutored to honor fittingly the power which this
sigil served. But it is not expedient to speak clearly
concerning this; and the real name of the sigil was, of
course, quite different from that which Kennaston had given
it in his romance.

So began an odd divided life for Felix Kennaston. At first
he put his half of the sigil in an envelope, which he hid in a
desk in the library, under a pile of his dead uncle's unused
bookplates; whence, when occasion served, it was taken out
in order that when held so as to reflect the lamplight—for
this was always necessary,—it might induce the desired
dream of Ettarre.

Later Kennaston thought of an expedient by which to

prolong his dreams. Nightly he lighted and set by his bedside a stump of candle. The tiny flame, after he had utilized its reflection, would harmlessly burn out while his body slept with a bit of metal in one hand; and he would be freed of Felix Kennaston for eight hours uninterruptedly. To have left an electric-light turned on until he awakened, would in the end have exposed him to detection and the not-impossible appointment of a commission in lunacy; and he recognized the potentialities of such mischance with frank distaste. As affairs sped, however, he could without great difficulty buy his candles in secret. He was glad now to be well-to-do, if only because, as one result of their materially bettered fortunes, he and his wife had separate bedrooms.

CHAPTER **18**

Treats of a Prelate and, in Part, of Pigeons

THE DAY-LIT part of Kennaston's life was largely devoted to writing *The Tinctured Veil*,—that amazing performance which he subsequently gave to a bewildered world. And for the rest, his waking life went on in the old round.

But this is not—not, save by way of an occasional parenthesis,—a chronicle of Felix Kennaston's doings in the flesh. You may find all that in Mr. Froser's *Biography*. Flippant, inefficient, and moody, Felix Kennaston was not in the flesh particularly engaging; and in writing this record it is necessary to keep his fat corporeal personality in the background as much as may be possible, lest this workaday mask, of unamiable flesh and mannerisms, should cause you, as it so often induced us of Lichfield, to find the man repellent, and nothing more.

Now it befell that this spring died Bishop Arkwright—of the Cathedral of the Bleeding Heart,—and many dignitaries of his faith journeyed to Lichfield to attend the funeral. Chief among these was a prelate who very long ago had lived in Lichfield, when he was merely a bishop. Kennaston was no little surprised to receive a note informing him that this eminent churchman would be pleased to see Mr. Felix Kennaston that evening at the Bishop's House.

The prelate sat alone in a sparsely furnished, rather dark, and noticeably dusty room. He was like a lean effigy carved in time-yellowed ivory, and his voice was curiously ingratiating. Kennaston recognized with joy that this old man talked like a person in a book, in completed sentences and picked phrases, instead of employing the fragmentary verbal shorthand of ordinary Lichfieldian conversation: and Kennaston, to whom the slovenliness of fairly cultured people's daily talk was always a mystery and an irritant, fell with promptitude into the same tone.

The prelate, it developed, had when he lived in Lichfield known Kennaston's dead uncle,—"for whom I had the highest esteem, and whose friendship I valued most dearly." He hoped that Kennaston would pardon the foibles of old age and overlook this trespass upon Kennaston's time. For the prelate had, he said, really a personal interest in the only surviving relative of his dead friend.

"There is a portrait of you, sir, in my library,—very gorgeous, in full canonicals,—just as my uncle left the room," said Kennaston, all at sea.

But the prelate had begun to talk—amiably, and in the most commonplace fashion conceivable,—of his former life in Lichfield, and of the folk who had lived there then, and to ask questions about their descendants, which Kennaston answered as he best could. The whole affair was puzzling Kennaston, for he could think of no reason why this frail ancient gentleman should have sent for a stranger, even though that stranger were the nephew of a dead friend, just that they might discuss trivialities.

So their talking veered, as it seemed, at random. . . .

"Yes, I was often a guest at Alcluid—a very beautiful home it was in those days, famed, as I remember, for the many breeds of pigeons which your uncle amused himself by maintaining. I suppose that you also raise white pigeons, my son?"

Kennaston saw that the prelate now held a small square mirror in his left hand. "No, sir," Kennaston answered evenly; "there were a great many about the place when it came into our possession; but we have never gone in very seriously for farming."

"The pigeon has so many literary associations that I should have thought it would appeal to a man of letters," the prelate continued. "I ought to have said earlier perhaps that I read *Men Who Loved Alison* with great interest and enjoyment. It is a notable book. Yet in dealing with the sigil of Scoteia—or so at least it seemed to me,—you touched upon subjects which had better be left undisturbed. There are drugs, my son, which work much good in the hands of the skilled physician, but cannot without danger be entrusted to the vulgar."

He spoke gently; yet it appeared to Kennaston a threat was voiced.

"Sir," Kennaston began, "I must tell you that in writing of the sigil—as I called it,—I designed to employ only such general terms as romance ordinarily accords to talismans. All I wrote—I thought,—was sheer invention. It is true I found by accident a bit of metal, from which I derived the idea of my so-called sigil's appearance. That bit of metal was to me then just a bit of metal; nor have I any notion, even to-day, as to how it came to be lying in one of my own garden-paths."

Kennaston paused.

The prelate nodded. "It is always interesting to hear whence makers of creative literature draw their material," he stated.

"Since then, sir, by the drollest of coincidences," said Kennaston, as unconcernedly as he could manage, "a famous personage has spoken to me in almost the identical words you employed this evening, as to the sigil of Scoteia. The coincidence, sir, lay less in what was said than in the apparently irrelevant allusion to white pigeons which the personage too made, and the little mirror which he too held as he spoke. Can you not see, sir," Kennaston asked gaily, "to what wild imaginings the coincidence tempts a weaver of romance? I could find it in my heart to believe it the cream of an ironic jest that you great ones of the earth have tested me with a password, mistakenly supposing that I, also, was initiate. I am tempted to imagine some secret understanding, some hidden cooperancy, by which you strengthen or, possibly, have attained your power. Confess, sir, is not the coincidence a droll one?"

Now Kennaston spoke lightly, but his heart was beating fast.

"It is remarkable enough," the prelate conceded, smiling. He asked the name of the personage whom coincidence linked with him, and being told it, chuckled.

"I do not think it very odd he carried a mirror," the prelate considered. "He lives before a mirror, and behind a megaphone. I confess—*mea culpa!*—I often find my little looking-glass a convenience, in making sure all is right before I go into the pulpit. Not a few men in public life, I believe, carry such mirrors," the prelate continued, slowly. "But you, I take it, have no taste for public life?"

"I can assure you—" Kennaston began.

"Think well, my son! Suppose, for one mad instant, that your wild imaginings were not wholly insane? suppose that you had accidentally stumbled upon enough of a certain secret to make it simpler to tell you the whole mystery? Cannot a trained romancer conceive what you might hope for then?"

Very still it was in the dark room. . . .

Kennaston was horribly frightened. "I can assure you, sir, that even then I would prefer my peaceful lazy life and my dreams. I have not any aptitude for action."

"Ah, well," the prelate estimated; "it is scarcely a churchman's part to play *advocatus mundi*. Believe me, I would not tempt you from your books. And for our dreams, I have always held heretically, we are more responsible than for our actions, since it is what we are, uninfluenced, that determines our dreams." He seemed to meditate. "I shall not tempt you, therefore, to tell me the whole truth concerning that bit of metal."

"Oh, as to that, sir—!"

"You said just now," the older man continued, equably,

" 'that bit of metal was to me then just a bit of metal.' There can be much virtue in a 'then.' So I suspect quite candidly, you are keeping something back. But, in doing so, you exercise a privilege common to both of us."

"At least," said Kennaston, "we will hope my poor wits may not be shaken by any more—coincidences."

"I am tolerably certain," quoth the prelate, with an indulgent smile, "that there will be no more coincidences."

Then he gave Kennaston his stately blessing; and Felix Kennaston went back to his life of dreams.

CHAPTER 19

Local Laws of
Nephelococcygia

THERE WAS NO CONTINUITY in these dreams save that Ettarre was in each of them. A dream would usually begin with some lightheaded topsyturviness, as when Kennaston found himself gazing forlornly down at his remote feet,—having grown so tall that they were yards away from him and he was afraid to stand up,—or when thin men in black hoods carefully explained the importance of the task set him by quoting fragments of the multiplication tables, or when a bull who happened to be the King of Spain was pursuing him through a city of blind people. But presently, as dregs settle a little by a little in a glass of water and leave it clear, his dream-world would become rational and compliant with familiar natural laws, and Ettarre would be there,—desirable above all other contents of the universe, and not to be touched under penalty of ending all.

Sometimes they would be alone in places which he did not recognize, sometimes they would be living, under the Stuarts or the Valois or the Caesars, or other dynasties long since unkingdomed, human lives whose obligations and imbroglios affected Horvendile and Ettarre to much that half-serious concern with which one follows the action of a romance or a well-acted play; for it was perfectly understood between Horvendile and Ettarre that they were involved in the affairs of a dream.

Ettarre seemed to remember nothing of the happenings Kennaston had invented in his book. And Guiron and Maugis d'Aigremont and Count Emmerick and the other people in *The Audit at Storisende*—once more to give *Men Who Loved Alison* its original title,—were names that rang familiar to her somehow, she confessed, but without her knowing why. And so, Kennaston came at last to comprehend that perhaps the Ettarre he loved was not the heroine of his book inexplicably vivified; but, rather, that in the book he had, just as inexplicably, drawn a blurred portrait of the Ettarre he loved, that ageless lovable and loving woman of whom all poets had been granted fitful broken glimpses,—dimly prefiguring her advent into his life too, with pallid and feeble visionings. But of this he was not ever sure; nor did he greatly care, now that he had his dreams.

There was, be it repeated, no continuity in these dreams save that Ettarre was in each of them; that alone they had in common: but each dream conformed to certain general laws. For instance, there was never any confusion of time,—that is, a dream extended over precisely the amount of time he actually slept, so that each dream-life was limited to some eight hours or thereabouts. No dream was ever iterated, nor did he ever twice find himself in the same surroundings as touched chronology; thus, he was often in Paris and Constantinople and Alexandria and Rome and London, revisiting even the exact spot, the very street-corner, which had figured in some former dream; but as terrestrial time went, the events of his first dream would either have happened years ago or else not be due to happen until a great while later.

He never dreamed of absolutely barbaric or orderless epochs, nor of happenings (so far as he could ascertain) elsewhere than in Europe and about the Mediterranean coasts; even within these confines his dreams were as a rule restricted to urban matters, rarely straying beyond city walls: his hypothesis in explanation of these facts was curious, but too finespun to be here repeated profitably.

For a while Kennaston thought these dreams to be bits of lives he had lived in previous incarnations; later he was inclined to discard this view. He never to his knowledge lived through precisely the same moment in two different capacities and places; but more than once he came within a few years of doing this, so that even had he died immediately after the earlier-timed dream, it would have been impossible for him to have been reborn and reach the age he had attained in that dream whose period was only a trifle later. In his dreams Kennaston's age varied slightly, but was almost always in pleasant proximity to twenty-five. Thus, he was in Jerusalem on the day of the Crucifixion and was aged about twenty-three; yet in another dream he was at Capreae when Tiberius died there, seven years afterward, and Kennaston was then still in the early twenties: and, again, he was in London, at Whitehall, in 1649, and at Vaux-le-Vicomte near Fontainebleau in 1661, being on each occasion twenty-three or -four. Kennaston could suggest no explanation of this.

He often regretted that he was never in any dream anybody of historical prominence, so that he could have found out what became of him after the dream ended. But though he sometimes talked with notable persons,—inwardly gloating meanwhile over his knowledge of what would be the outcome of their warfaring or statecraft, and of the manner and even the hour of their deaths,—he himself seemed fated, as a rule, never to be anyone of importance in the world's estimation. Indeed, as Kennaston cheerfully recognized, his was not a temperament likely to succeed, as touched material matters, in any imaginable state of society; there was not, and never had been, any workaday world in which—as he had said at Storisende,—he and his like would not, in so far as temporal prizes were concerned, appear to waste at loose ends and live futilely. Then, moreover, in each dream he was woefully hampered by inability to recall preceding events in the life he was then leading, which handicap doomed him to redoubled inefficiencies. But that did not matter now, in view of his prodigal recompenses. . . .

It was some while before the man made the quaint

discovery that in these dreams he did not in any way resemble Felix Kennaston physically. They were astray in an autumn forest, resting beside a small fire which he had kindled in the shelter of a boulder, when Ettarre chanced to speak of his brown eyes, and thereby to perplex him. But there was in this dream nothing which would reflect his countenance; and it was later, in Troy Town (Laomedon ruled the city then, and Priam they saw as a lad playing at marbles in a paved courtyard, where tethered oxen watched him over curiously painted mangers), that Kennaston looked into a steel mirror, framed with intertwined ivory serpents that had emeralds for eyes, and found there a puzzled stranger.

Thus it was he discovered that in these dreams he was a tall lean youngster, with ruddy cheeks, wide-set brown eyes, and a smallish head covered with crisp tight-curling dark-red hair; nor did his appearance ever change, save only once, in any subsequent dream. What he saw was so different from the pudgy pasty man of forty-odd who, he knew, lay at this moment in Felix Kennaston's bed, breathing heavily and clasping a bit of metal in his pudgy hand, that the stranger in the mirror laughed appreciatively.

CHAPTER **20**

Of Divers Fleshly Riddles

A LITTLE BY A LITTLE he was beginning to lose interest in that pudgy pasty man of forty-odd who was called Felix Kennaston, and to handle his affairs more slackly. Once or twice Kennaston caught his wife regarding him furtively, with a sort of anxious distrust. . . .

Let there be no mistake here: Felix Kennaston had married a woman admirably suited to him, and he had never regretted that act. Nor with the advent of Ettarre, did he regret it: and never at any time would he have considered separating his diurnal existence from that of his thin, beady-eyed, capable wife, with graver seriousness than he would have accorded, say, to a rambling notion of being gripped some day in a trap and having no way to escape save by cutting off one of his feet. His affection for Kathleen was well-founded, proved, and understood; but, as it happens, this narrative does not chance to deal with that affection. And besides, what there was to tell concerning Kennaston's fondness for his wife was duly set forth years ago.

Meanwhile, it began vaguely to be rumored among Kennaston's associates that he drank more than was good for him; and toward "drugs" also sped the irresponsible arrows of surmise. He himself noticed, without much interest, that daily he, who had once been garrulous, was growing more chary of speech; and that his attention was apt to wander when the man's or woman's face before him spoke at any length. These shifting faces talked of wars and tariffs and investments and the weather and committee-meetings, and of having seen So-and-so and of So-and-so's having said this or that, and it all seemed of importance to the wearers of these faces; so that he made pretense to listen, patiently. What did it matter?

It did not matter a farthing, he considered, for he had cheated life of its main oppression, which is loneliness. Now at last Felix Kennaston could unconcernedly acknowledge that human beings develop graveward in continuous solitude.

His life until this time had been in the main normal, with its due share of normal intimacies with parents, kinsmen, friends, a poet's ordinary allotment of sweethearts, and, chief of all, with his wife. No one of these people, as he reflected in a comminglement of yearning and complacency, had ever comprehended the real Felix Kennaston as he existed, in all his hampered strugglings and meannesses, his inadequacies and his divine unexercised potentialities.

And he, upon the other hand, knew nothing of these people with any certainty. Pettifoggeries were too easily practised in speech or gesture, emotions were too often feigned or overcolored in expression, and unpopular thoughts were too instinctively dissembled, as he forlornly knew by his own conduct of daily life, for him to put very zealous faith in any information gained through his slender fallible five senses; and it was the cream of the jest that through these five senses lay his only means of getting any information whatsoever.

All that happened to him, he considered, happened inside his skull. Nothing which happened in the big universe affected him in the least except as it roused certain forces lodged in his skull. His life consisted of one chemical change after another, haphazardly provoked in some three pounds of fibrous matter tucked inside his skull. And so, people's heads took on a new interest; how was one to guess what was going on in those queer round boxes, inset with eyes, as people so glibly called certain restive and glinting things that moved in partial independence of their setting, and seemed to have an individual vitality,—in those queer round boxes out of which an uncanny vegetation, that people, here again, so glibly and unwonderingly called hair, was sprouting as if from the soil of a planet?

Perhaps—he mused,—perhaps in reality all heads were like isolated planets, with impassable space between each and its nearest neighbor. You read in the newspapers every once in a while that, because of one or another inexplicable phenomenon, Mars was supposed to be attempting to communicate with the earth; and perhaps it was in just such blurred and unsatisfactory fashion that what happened in one human head was signaled to the lonely inhabitant of yet another one of those queer round boxes, on those rare occasions when the signal was despatched in entire good faith. Yes, a perpetual isolation, for all the fretful and vain strivings of humanity against such loneliness, was probably a perdurable law in all other men's lives, precisely as it had been in his own life until the coming of Ettarre.

CHAPTER **21**

In Pursuit of a Whisper

NIGHTLY HE WENT adventuring with Ettarre: and they saw the cities and manners of many men, to an extent undreamed-of by Ithaca's mundivagant king; and among them even those three persons who had most potently influenced human life.

For once, in an elongated room with buff-colored walls—having scarlet hangings over its windows, and seeming larger than it was in reality, because of its many mirrors,—they foregathered with Napoleon, on the evening following his coronation: the emperor of half-Europe was fretting over an awkward hitch in the day's ceremony, caused by his sisters' attempt to avoid carrying the Empress Josephine's train; and he was grumbling because the old French families continued to ignore him, as a parvenu. All in all, the Emperor had got no pleasure out of his day's work.

In a neglected orchard, sunsteeped and made drowsy by the murmur of bees, they talked with Shakespeare: the playwright, his nerves the worse for the preceding night's potations, was peevishly complaining of the meager success of his later comedies, he was worrying over Lord Pembroke's neglect of him, and he was trying to concoct a masque in the style of fat Ben Jonson, since that was evidently what the theater-patronizing public wanted; and, working thus against the grain, Shakespeare had got not any pleasure out of his day's work.

Then they were with Pontius Pilate in Jerusalem, on the evening of a day when the sky had been black and the earth had trembled; and Pilate, benevolent and replete with supper, was explaining the latest theories concerning eclipses and earthquakes to his little boy, and he was chuckling with fond pride in the youngster's intelligent questions, because Pontius Pilate was exceedingly well pleased with his day's work.

These three were a few among the prominent worthies of remoter days whom Kennaston was enabled to view as they appeared in the flesh; but, as a rule, chance thrust him into the company of mediocre people living ordinary lives amid surroundings which seemed outlandish to him, but to them a matter of course. And everywhere, in every age, it seemed to him, men stumbled amiable and shatterpated through a jungle of miracles, blind to its wonderfulness, and intent to gain a little money, food and sleep, a trinket or two, some rare snatched fleeting moments of rantipole laughter, and at the last a decent bed to die in. He, and he only, it seemed to Felix Kennaston, could see the jungle and all its awe-inspiring beauty, wherethrough men scurried like feeble-minded ants.

He often wondered whether any other man had been so licensed as himself; and prowling, as he presently did, in odd byways of printed matter,—for he found the library of his predecessor at Alcluid a mine rich-veined with strangenesses,—Kennaston lighted on much that appeared to him significant. Even such apparently unrelated matters as the doctrine of metempsychosis, all the grotesque literature of witches, sorcerers, and familiar spirits, and of muses who actually prompted artistic composition with audible voices, were beginning to fall into cloudily-discerned interlocking. Kennaston read much nowadays in his dead uncle's books; and he often wished that, even at the expense of Felix Kennaston's being reduced again to poverty, it were possible to revivify the man who had amassed and read these books. Kennaston wanted to talk with him.

Meanwhile, Kennaston read of Endymion and Numa, of Iason and Anchises, of Tannhäuser, and Foulques Plantagenet, and Raymondin de la Forêt, and Olger Danske, and other mortal men to whom old legend-weavers, as if wistfully, accredited the love of immortal mistresses,—and he read, too, of less fortunate nympholepts, frail babbling planet-stricken folk, who had spied by accident upon an unhuman loveliness, and so, must pine away consumed by foiled desire of a beauty which the homes and cities and the tilled places of men did not afford, and life did not bring forth sufficingly. He read Talmudic tales of Sulieman-ben-Daoud,—even in name transfigured out of any resemblance to an amasser of reliable axioms,—that proud luxurious despot, "who went daily to the comeliest of the spirits for wisdom"; and of Arthur and the Lady Nimuë; and of Thomas of Ercildoune, whom the Queen of Faëry drew from the merchants' market-place with ambiguous kindnesses; and of John Faustus, who "through fantasies and deep cogitations" was enabled to woo successfully a woman that died long before his birth, and so won to his love, as the book recorded, "this stately pearl of Greece, fair Helena, the wife to King Menelaus."

And, as has been said, the old idea of muses who actually prompted artistic composition, with audible voices, took on another aspect. He came to suspect that other creative writers had shared such a divided life as his was now, for of this he seemed to find traces here and there. Coleridge offered at once an arresting parallel. Yes, Kennaston reflected; and Coleridge had no doubt spoken out in the first glow of wonder, astounded into a sort of treason, when he revealed how he wrote *Kubla Khan;* so that thus perhaps Coleridge had told far more concerning the origin of this particular poem than he ever did as to some of his later compositions. Then, also, I have a volume of Herrick from Kennaston's library with curious comments penciled therein, relative to *Lovers How They Come and Part* and to *His Mistress Calling Him to Elysium;* a copy of Marlowe's *Tragical History of Doctor Faustus* is similarly annotated; and on a fly-leaf in Forster's *Life of Charles Dickens,* apropos of passages in the first chapter of the ninth book, Kennaston has inscribed strange speculations very ill suited to general reading. All that Kennaston cared to print, however, concerning the hypothesis he eventually evolved, you can find in *The Tinctured Veil,* where he has nicely refrained from too-explicit writing, and—of course—does not anywhere point-blank refer to his personal experiences.

Then Kennaston ran afoul of the Rosicrucians, and their quaint dogmas, which appeared so preposterous at first, took on vital meanings presently; and here too he seemed to surprise the cautious whispering of men who neither cared nor dared to speak with candor of all they knew. It seemed to him he understood that whispering which was everywhere apparent in human history; for he too was initiate.

He wondered very often about his uncle. . . .

CHAPTER **22**

Of Truisms:
Treated Reasonably

HE SEEMED, indeed, to find food for wonder everywhere. It was as if he had awakened from a dragging nightmare of life made up of unimportant tasks and tedious useless little habits, to see life as it really was, and to rejoice in its exquisite wonderfulness.

How poignantly strange it was that life could afford him nothing save consciousness of the moment immediately at hand! Memory and anticipation, whatsoever else they might do,—and they had important uses, of course, in rousing emotion,—yet did not deal directly with reality. What you regretted, or were proud of, having done yesterday was no more real now than were the deeds of Caesar Borgia or St. Paul; and what you looked forward to within the half-hour was as non-existent as the senility of your unborn great-grandchildren. Never was man brought into contact with reality save through the evanescent emotions and sensations of that single moment, that infinitesimal fraction of a second, which was passing now. This commonplace, so simple and so old, bewildered Kennaston when he came unreservedly to recognize its truth. . . .

To live was to be through his senses conscious of a restricted number of these fractions of a second, one by one. Success in life, then, had nothing to do with bank-accounts or public office, or any step toward increasing the length of one's obituary notices, but meant, instead, to be engrossed utterly by many, by as many as was possible, of these instants. And complete success in life required a finding, in these absorbing instants, of employment for every faculty he possessed. It was for this that Kennaston had always vaguely longed; and to this, if only in dreams, he now attained.

If only in dreams! he debated: why, and was he not conscious, now, in his dreams, of every moment as it fled?

And corporeal life in banks and ballrooms and legislative
halls and palaces, nowhere had anything more than that to
offer mortal men.

It is not necessary to defend his course of reasoning; to
the contrary, its fallacy is no less apparent than its
conduciveness to unbusinesslike conclusions. But it is
highly necessary to tell you that, according to Felix
Kennaston's account, now, turn by turn, he was in
Horvendile's person rapt by nearly every passion, every
emotion, the human race has ever known. True, throughout
these dramas into which chance plunged him, in that he
knew always he was dreaming, he was at once performer
and spectator; but he played with the born actor's
zest,—feeling his part, as people say,—and permitting the
passion he portrayed to possess him almost completely.

Almost completely, be it repeated; for there was invariably a sufficient sense of knowing he was only dreaming to
prevent entire abandonment to the raw emotion. Kennaston
preferred it thus. He preferred in this more comely way to
play with human passions, rather than, as seemed the vulgar
use, to consent to become their battered plaything.

It pleased him, too, to be able to have done with such
sensations and emotions as did not interest him; for he had
merely to touch Ettarre, and the dream ended. In this
fashion he would very often terminate an existence which
was becoming distasteful,—resorting debonairly to this sort
of suicide, and thus dismissing an era's social orderings and
its great people as toys that, when played with, had failed to
amuse Felix Kennaston.

PART FOUR

**Which travels, roundabout,
to edifying and safe conclusions**

"But there were dreams to sell
Ill didst thou buy:
Life is a dream, they tell,
Waking to die.

"Dreaming a dream to prize,
Is wishing ghosts to rise;
And, if I had the spell
To call the buried—well,
Which one would I?"

CHAPTER 23

Economic Considerations
of Piety

AS HAS BEEN SAID, Kennaston read much curious matter in his dead uncle's library. . . . But most books—even Felix Kennaston's own little books,—did not seem now to be affairs of heavy moment. For once abed, clasping his gleaming broken bit of metal, then the truthful history of all that had ever happened was, instead, Kennaston's library. It was not his to choose from what volume or on which page thereof he would read; accident, as it seemed, decided that: but the chance-opened page lay unblurred before him, and he saw it with a clarity denied to other men of his generation.

Kennaston stood by the couch of Tiberius Caeser as he lay ill at Capreae. Beside the Emperor hung a memorable painting, by Parrhasius, which represented the virgin Atalanta in the act of preserving her virginity by according oral assuagements to her lover's ardor.

Charicles, a Greek physician, was telling the Emperor of a new religious sect that had arisen in Judea, and of the persecutions which these disciples of Christus were enduring. Old Caesar listened, made grave clucking noises of disapproval, and said forthwith:

"It is, instead, a religion that should be fostered. The man preached peace. It is what my father before me strove for, what I have striven for, what my successors must strive for. Peace alone may preserve Rome: the empire is too large, a bubble blown so big and tenuous that the first shock will disrupt it in suds. Pilate did well to crucify the man, else we could not have made a God of him; but the persecution of these followers of Christus must cease. This Nazarene preached the same doctrine that I have always preached. I shall build him a temple. The rumors concerning him lack novelty, it is true: this God born of a mortal woman is the old legend of Dionysos and Mithra and Hercules, a little pulled about; Gautama also was tempted in a wilderness; Prometheus served long ago as man's scapegoat under divine anger; and the cult of Pollux and Castor, and of Adonis, has made these resurrection stories hackneyed. In fine, Charicles, you have brought me a woefully inartistic jumble of old tales; but the populace prefers old tales, they delight to be told what they have heard already. I shall certainly build Christus a temple."

So he ran on, devising the reception of Christ into the Roman pantheon, as a minor deity at first, and thence, if the receipts at his temple justified it, to be raised to greater eminence. Tiberius saw large possibilities in the worship of this new God, both from a doctrinal and a money-making standpoint. Then Caesar yawned, and ordered that a company of his Spintriae be summoned to his chamber, to amuse him with their unnatural diversions.

But Charicles had listened in horror, for he was secretly a Christian, and knew that the blood of the martyrs is the seed of the church. He foresaw that, without salutary discouragement, the worship of Christus would never amount to more than the social fad of a particular season, just as that of Cybele and that of Ela-Gabal had been modish in different years; and would afterward dwindle, precisely as these cults had done, into shrugged-at old-fashionedness. Then, was it not written that they only were assuredly blessed who were persecuted for righteousness' sake?—Why, martyrdom was the one certain road to Heaven; and a religion which is patronized by potentates, obviously, breeds no martyrs.

So Charicles mingled poison in Caesar's drink, that Caesar might die, and crazed Caligula succeed him, to put all Christians to the sword. And Charicles young Caius Caesar Caligula—Child of the Camp, Father of Armies, Beloved of the Gods,—killed first of all.

Then a lean man, white-robed, and clean-shaven as to his head, was arranging a complicated toy. He labored in a gray-walled room, lit only by one large circular window opening upon the sea. There was an alcove in this room, and in the alcove stood a large painted statue.

This prefigured a crowned woman, in bright parti-colored garments of white and red and yellow, under a black mantle embroidered with small sparkling stars. Upon the woman's forehead was a disk, like a round glittering mirror; seen closer, it was engraved with tiny characters, and Kennaston viewed it with a thrill of recognition. To the woman's right were vipers rising from the earth, and to the left were stalks of ripe corn, all in their proper colors. In one hand she carried a golden boat, from which a coiled asp raised its head threateningly. From the other hand dangled a cluster of slender metal rods, which were not a part of the statue, but were loosely attached to it, so that the least wind caused them to move and jangle. There was nothing whatever in the gray-walled room save this curious gleaming statue and the lean man and the mechanical toy on which he labored.

He explained its workings, willingly enough. See now! you kindled a fire in this little cube-shaped box. The air inside expanded through this pipe into the first jar of water, and forced the water out, through this other pipe, into this tiny bucket. The bucket thus became heavier and heavier, till its weight at last pulled down the string by which the bucket was swung over a pulley, and so, moved this lever.

Oh, yes, the notion was an old one; the priest admitted he had copied the toy from one made by Heron of Alexandria, who died years ago. Still, it was an ingenious trifle: moreover—and here was the point,—enlarge the scale, change the cube shaped box into the temple altar, fasten the lever to the temple doors, and you had the mechanism for a miracle. People had only to offer burnt sacrifices to the Goddess, and before their eyes the All-Mother, the holy and perpetual preserver of the human race, would stoop to material thaumaturgy, and would condescend to animate her sacred portals, so that they would unclose without human agency and would thus open her shrine to all the faithful who had attested the soundness of their faith by honoring her with burnt sacrifices.

"We very decidedly need some striking miracle to advertise our temple," he told Kennaston. "Folk are flocking

like sheep after these barbarous new Galilean heresies. But
the All-Mother is compassionate to human frailty; and this
device will win back many erring feet to the true way."

And Kennaston saw there were tears in this man's dark
sad eyes. The trickster was striving to uphold the faith of his
fathers; and in the attempt he had constructed a practicable
steam-engine.

CHAPTER 24

Deals with Pen Scratches

THEN KENNASTON was in Alexandria when John the
Grammarian pleaded with the victorious Arabian general
Amrou to spare the royal library, which at this period was
the sole repository of many of the masterworks of Greek
and Roman literature.

But Amrou only laughed, with a practical man's contempt
for such matters. Amrou then said, as became a devout
Mussulman:

"The Koran contains all that is necessary to salvation: if
these books teach as the Koran teaches they are superfluous;
if they contain anything contrary to the Koran they ought to
be destroyed. Let them be used as fuel for the public
baths."

And this was done. . . . Curious, very curious, it was to
Kennaston, to witness this utilitarian employment of a
nation's literature; and it moved him strangely. For he had
come at this season to believe that individual acts can count
for nothing, in the outcome of things. Whatever might
happen upon earth, affected infinitesimally, if it affected at
all, the revealed universe of which this planet was a part so
inconceivably tiny. To figure out the importance in this
universe of the deeds of one or another nation temporarily
clustering on earth's surface—when you considered that
neither the doings of Assyria or of Rome, nor of any other

kingdom, had ever at any period extended from earth's surface by more than a few hundred yards,—was a computing far too delicate for human reason. For human faculties to attempt to estimate the individuals of this nation, in the light of the relative importance of their physical antics while living, was purely and simply ridiculous. To assume, as did so many well-meaning persons, that Omniscience devoted eternity to puzzling out just these minutiae, seemed at the mildest to postulate in Omniscience a queer mania for trivialities.

No: with the passage of time, whatever a man had done whether for good or evil, with the man's bodily organs, left the man's parish unaffected: only man's thoughts and dreams could outlive him, in any serious sense, and these might survive with perhaps augmenting influence: so that Kennaston had come to think artistic creation in words —since marble and canvas inevitably perished,—was the one, possibly, worth-while employment of human life. But here was a crude corporal deed which bluntly destroyed thoughts, and annihilated dreams by wholesale. To Kennaston this seemed the one real tragedy that could be staged on earth. . . .

Curious, very curious, it was to Kennaston, to see the burning of sixty-three plays written by Aeschylus, of a hundred and six by Sophocles, and of fifty-five by Euripides,—masterworks eternally lost, which, as Kennaston knew, the world would affect to deplore eternally, whatever might be the world's real opinion in the matter.

But of these verbal artificers something at least was to endure. They would fare better than Agathon and Ion and Achaeus, their admitted equals in splendor, whose whole life-work was passing, at the feet of Horvendile, into complete oblivion. There, too, were perishing all the writings of the Pleiad,—the noble tragedies of Homerus, and Sositheus, and Lycophron, and Alexander, and Philiscus, and Sosiphanes, and Dionysides. All the great comic poets, too, were burned pellmell with these,—Telecleides, Hermippus, Eupolis, Antiphanes, Ameipsas, Lysippus, and Menander,—"whom nature mimicked," as the phrase was. And here, posting to obliteration, went likewise Thespis, and Pratinas, and Phrynichus,—and Choerilus, whom cultured persons had long ranked with Homer. Nothing was to remain of any of these save the bare name, and even this would be known only to pedants. All these, spurred by the poet's ageless monomania, had toiled toward, and had attained, the poet's ageless goal—to write perfectly of beautiful happenings: and of this action's normal by-product, which is immortality in the mouths and minds of succeeding generations, all these were being robbed, by the circumstance that parchment is inflammable.

Here was beauty, and wit, and learning, and genius, being wasted—quite wantonly,—never to be recaptured, never to be equalled again (despite the innumerable painstaking penmen destined to fret the hearts of unborn wives), and never, in the outcome, to be thought of as a very serious loss to anybody, after all. . . .

These book-rolls burned with great rapidity, crackling cheerily as the garnered wisdom of the elder Cato's octogenarian life dissolved in puffs of smoke, and the wit of Sosipater blazed for the last time in heating a pint of water. . . . But then in Parma long afterward Kennaston observed a monk erasing a song of Sappho's from a parchment on which the monk meant to inscribe a feeble little Latin hymn of his own composition; in an obscure village near Alexandria Kennaston saw the only existent copy of the *Mimes* of Herondas crumpled up and used as packing for a mummy-case; in the tidiest of old English kitchens Kennaston watched thrifty Betty Baker, then acting as cook for Warburton the antiquary, destroy in making pie-crust the unique manuscript copies of some fifty plays, among which were never-printed tragedies by Marlowe and Cyril Tourneur and George Chapman, and comedies by Middleton and Greene and Dekker, and—rather drolly, —those same three dramas which Shakespeare, when he talked with Horvendile in the orchard, had asserted to perpetuate, upon the whole, the most excellent fruit of Shakespeare's ripened craftsmanship.

Yet—conceding Heaven to be an actual place, and attainment of its felicities to be the object of human life,—Kennaston could not, after all, detect any fault in Amroụ's logic. Aesthetic considerations could, in that event, but lead to profitless time-wasting where every moment was precious.

CHAPTER **25**

By-Products of Rational Endeavor

THEN AGAIN Kennaston stood in a stone-walled apartment, like a cell, wherein he saw a furnace and much wreckage. A contemplative friar was regarding the disorder about him with disapproval, the while he sucked at two hurt fingers.

"There can be no doubt that Old Legion conspires to hinder the great work," he considered.

"And what is the great work, father?" Kennaston asked him.

"To find the secret of eternal life, my son. What else is lacking? Man approaches to God in all things save this, *Imaginis imago,* created after God's image. But as yet, by reason of his mortality, man shudders in a world that is arrayed against him. Thus, the heavens threaten with winds and lightnings, with plague-breeding meteors and the unfriendly aspect of planets; the big seas molest with waves and inundations, stealthily drowning cities overnight, and sucking down tall navies as a child gulps sugarplums; whereas how many plants and gums and seeds bear man's destruction in their tiny hearts! what soulless beasts of the field and of the wood are everywhere enleagued in endless feud against him, with tusks and teeth, with nails and claws and venomous stings, made sharp for man's demolishment! Thus all struggle miserably, like hunted persons under a sentence of death that may, at best, be avoided for a little while. And manifestly, this is not as it should be."

"Yet I much fear it is so ordered, father."

The old man said testily: "I repeat, for your better comfort, there can be no doubt that Satan alone conspires to hinder the great work. No; it would be abuse of superstition to conceive, as would be possible for folk of slender courage, that the finger of Heaven has to-day unloosed this destruction, to my bodily hurt and spiritual admonition."

Kennaston could see, though, that the speaker half believed this might be exactly what had happened. Meanwhile the old lean friar continued:

"—For I am about no vaunting transgression of man's estate; I do but seek to recover his lost heritage. You will say to me, it is written that never shall any man be one day old in the sight of God?—Yet it is likewise written that unto God a thousand years are but one day. For one thousand years, then, may each man righteously hope to have death delay to enact the midwife to his second birth. It advantages not to contend that even in the heyday of patriarchs few approached to such longevity; for Moses, relinquishing to silence all save the progeny of Seth, nowhere directly tells us that some of the seed of Cain did not outlive Methuselah. Yea, and our common parent, Adam, was created in the mature age of man, which then fell not short of one hundred years, since at less antiquity did none of the antediluvian fathers beget issue, as did Adam in the same year breath was given him; and the years of Adam's life were nine hundred and thirty; whereby it is a reasonable conceit of learned persons to compute him to have exceeded a thousand years in age, if not in duration of existence. Now, it is written that we shall all die as Adam died; and caution should not scruple to affirm this is an excellent dark saying, prophetic of that day when no man need outdo Adam in celerity to put by his flesh."

Then Kennaston found the alchemist had been compounding nitrum of Memphis with sulphur, mixing in a little willow charcoal to make the whole more friable, and that the powder had exploded. The old man was now interested, less in the breakage, than in the horrible noise which this accident had occasioned.

"The mixture might be used in court-pageants and miracle-plays," he estimated, "to indicate the entrance of Satan, or the fall of Sodom, or Herod's descent into the Pit, and so on. Yes, I shall thriftily sell this secret, and so get money to go on with the great work."

Seeking to find the means of making life perpetual, he had accidentally discovered gunpowder.

Then at Valladolid an age-stricken seaman, wracked with gout, tossed in a mean bed and grumbled to bare walls. He, "the Admiral," was neglected by King Philip, the broth was unfit for a dog's supper, his son Diego was a laggard fool. Thus the old fellow mumbled.

Ingratitude everywhere! and had not he, "the Admiral"—"the Admiral of Mosquito Land," as damnable street-songs miscalled him, he whimpered, in a petulant gust of self-pity,—had not he found out at last a way by sea to the provinces of the Great Khan and the treasures of Cipango? Give him another fleet, and he would demonstrate what malignant fools were his enemies. He would convert the Khan from Greek heresies; or else let the Holy Inquisition be established in Cipango, the thumbscrew and the stake be fittingly utilized there *ad majoreum Dei gloriam,*—all should redound to the credit of King Philip, both temporal and celestial. And what wealth, too, a capable emissary would bring back to his Majesty,—what cargoes of raw silks, of gold and precious gems, ravished from Kanbalu and Taidu, those famed marvelous cities! . . . But there was only ingratitude and folly everywhere; the King was misled by wicked advisers; and the broth was cold as a king's heart.

Thus mumbled the broken adventurer, Cristoforo Colombo. He had doubled the world's size and resources, in his attempts to find some defenseless nation which could be plundered with impunity; and he was dying in ignorance of what his endeavors had achieved.

And Kennaston was at Blickling Hall when King Henry read the Pope's letter which threatened excommunication. "Nan, Nan," the King said, "this is a sorry business."

"Sire," says Mistress Boleyn, saucily, "and am I not worth a little abuse?"

"You deserve some quite certainly," he agrees; and his bright lecherous pig's eyes twinkled, and he guffawed.

"Defy the Pope, then, sire, and marry your true love. Let us snap fingers at Giulio de Medici—"

"Faith, and not every lass can bring eleven fingers to the task," the King put in.

She tweaked his fine gold beard, and Kennaston saw that upon her left hand there was really an extra finger.

"My own sweetheart," says she, "if you would have my person as much at your disposal as my heart is, we must part company with Rome. Then too, at the cost of a few Latin phrases, some foolish candle-snuffing and a little bell-ringing, you may take for your own all the fat abbey-lands in these islands, and sell them for a great deal of money," she pointed out.

So, between lust and greed, the King was persuaded. In the upshot, "because"—as was duly set forth to his lieges,—"a virtuous monarch ought to surround his throne with many peers of the worthiest of both sexes," therefore Mistress Anne Boleyn was created Marchioness of Pembroke, in her own right, with a reversion of the title and estates to her offspring, whether (as might best please Heaven's high wisdom) the King's well-beloved and most virtuous cousin should happen to bear legitimate children or bastards. True love provides against all, the King remarked.

Moreover, a pension of £1,000 per annum, with gold, silver and parcel-gilt plate to the value of £1,188, was likewise awarded her: and the King, by thus piously defying Romish error, earned the abbey-lands, as well as the key to to his Nan's bedchamber, and the eternal approbation of zealous Protestants, for thus inaugurating religious liberty.

CHAPTER 26

"Epper Si Muove"

THESE IRONIES Kennaston witnessed among many others, as he read in this or that chance-opened page from the past. Everywhere, it seemed to him, men had labored blindly, at flat odds with rationality, and had achieved everything of note by accident. Everywhere he saw reason to echo the cry of Maugis d'Aigremont,—"It is very strange how affairs fall out in this world of ours, so that a man may discern no plan or purpose anywhere."

Here was the astounding fact: the race did go forward; the race did achieve; and in every way the race grew better.

Progress through irrational and astounding blunders, whose outrageousness bedwarfed the wildest clichés of romance, was what Kennaston found everywhere. All this, then, also was foreplanned, just as all happenings at Storisende had been, in his puny romance; and the puppets, here too, moved as they thought of their own volition, but really in order to serve a dénouement in which many of them had not any personal part or interest. . . .

And always the puppets moved toward greater efficiency and comeliness. The puppet-shifter appeared to seek, at once, utility and artistic self-expression. So the protoplasm—that first imperceptible pinhead of living matter,—had become a fish; the fish had become a batrachian, the batrachian a reptile, the reptile a mammal; thus had the puppets continuously been reshaped, into more elaborate forms more captivating to the eye, until amiable and shatter-pated man stood erect in the world. And man, in turn, had climbed a long way from gorillaship, howsoever far he was as yet from godhead,—blindly moving always, like fish and reptile, toward unapprehended loftier goals.

But, just as men's lives came to seem to Kennaston like many infinitesimal threads woven into the pattern of human destiny, so Kennaston grew to suspect that the existence of mankind upon earth was but an incident in the unending struggle of life to find a home in the universe. Human inhabitancy was not even a very important phase in the world's history, perhaps; a scant score or so of centuries ago there had been no life on earth, and by and by the planet would be a silent, naked, frozen clod. Would this sphere then have served its real purpose of being, by having afforded foothold to life for a few aeons?

He could not tell. But Kennaston contemplated sidereal space full of such frozen worlds, where life seemed to have flourished for a while and to have been dispossessed,—and full, too, of glowing suns, with their huge satellites, all slowly cooling and congealing into fitness for life's occupancy. Life would tarry there also, he reflected; and thence also life would be evicted. For life was not a part of the universe, not a product of the universe at all perhaps, but, rather, an intruder into the cosmic machinery, which moved without any consideration of life's needs. Like a bird striving to nest in a limitless engine, insanely building among moving wheels and cogs and pistons and pulley-bands, whose moving toward their proper and intended purposes inevitably swept away each nest before completion,—so it might be that life passed from moving world to world, found transitory foothold, began to build, and was driven out.

What was it that life sought to rear?—what was the purpose of this endless endeavor, of which the hatching of an ant or the begetting of an emperor was equally a by-product? and of which the existence of Felix Kennaston was a manifestation past conceiving in its unimportance? Toward what did life aspire?—that force which moved in Felix Kennaston, and thus made Felix Kennaston also an intruder, a temporary visitor, in the big moving soulless mechanism of earth and water and planets and suns and interlocking solar systems?

"To answer that question must be my modest attempt," he decided. "In fine—why is a Kennaston? The query has a humorous ring, undoubtedly, in so far as it is no little suggestive of the spinning mouse that is the higher the fewer,—but, after all, it voices the sole question in which I personally am interested. . . ."

"Why is a Kennaston?" he asked himself,—thus whimsically voicing a real desire to know if human beings were intended for any especial purpose. Most of us find it more comfortable, upon the whole, to stave off such queries,—with the jest, a shrug, or a Scriptural quotation, as best suits personal taste; but Kennaston was "queer" enough to face the situation quite gravely. Here was he, the individual, very possibly placed on—at all events, infesting,—a particular planet for a considerable number of years; the planet was so elaborately constructed, so richly clothed with trees and valleys and uplands and running waters and multitudinary grass-blades, and the body that housed Felix Kennaston was so intricately wrought with tiny bones and veins and sinews, with sockets and valves and levers, and little hairs which grew upon the body like grass-blades about the earth, that it seemed unreasonable to suppose this much cunning mechanism had been set a-going aimlessly: and so, he often wondered if he was not, perhaps, expected to devote these years of human living to some intelligible purpose?

Religion, of course, assured him that the answer to his query was, in various books, explicitly written, in very dissimilar forms. But Kennaston could find little to attract him in any theory of the universe based upon direct revelations from Heaven. Conceding that divinity had actually stated so-and-so, from Sinai or Delphi or Mecca, and had been reported without miscomprehension or error, there was no particular reason for presuming that divinity had spoken veraciously: and, indeed, all available analogues went to show that nothing in nature dealt with its inferiors candidly. To liken the relationship to the intercourse of a father with his children, as did all revealed religions with queer uniformity, was at best a two-edged simile, in that it suggested a possible amiability of intention combined with inevitable duplicity. The range of an earthly father's habitual deceptions, embracing the sources of life and Christmas presents on one side and his own fallibility on the other, was wide enough to make the comparison suspicious. When fathers were at their worst they punished; and when in their kindliest and most expansive moods, why, then it was—precisely—that they told their children fairy-stories. It seemed to Kennaston, for a while, that all religions ended in this blind-alley.

To exercise for an allotted period divinely-recommended qualities known as virtues, and to be rewarded therefor, by an immortal score-keeper, appeared a rather childish performance all around. Yet every religion agreed in asserting that such was the course of human life at its noblest; and to believe that matters were thus arranged indisputably satisfied an innate craving of men's natures, as Kennaston was, perhaps uniquely, privileged to see for himself.

Under all theocracies the run of men proved much the same: as has been said, it was for the most part with quite ordinary people that Horvendile dealt in dreams. The Roman citizenry, for instance, he found did not devote existence, either under the Republic or the Empire, to shouting in unanimous response to metrical declamations,

and worrying over their own bare legs, nor did they in many
other ways conform to the best traditions of literature and of
the stage; nor did the Athenians corroborate their dramatists
by talking perpetually of the might of Zeus or Aphrodite,
any more than motormen and stockbrokers conversed
continually of the Holy Ghost. Substantial people everywhere worshiped at their accustomed temple at accustomed
intervals, and then put the matter out of mind, in precisely
the fashion of any reputable twentieth-century church-goer.

They had meanwhile their business-affairs, their sober
chats on weather probabilities, their staid diversions (which
everywhere bored them frightfully), their family jokes, their
best and second-best clothes, their flirtations, their petty
snobbishness, and their perfectly irrational faith in Omnipotence and in the general kindliness of Omnipotence,—all
these they had, and made play with, to round out living.
Ritualistic worship everywhere seemed to be of the nature
of a conscious outing, of a conscious departure from
everyday life; it was generally felt that well-balanced
people would not permit such jaunts to interfere with their
business-matters or home-ties; but there was no doubt men
did not like to live without religion and religion's promise
of a less trivial and more ordered and symmetrical existence
tomorrow.

Meanwhile, men were to worry, somehow, through
to-day,—doing as infrequent evil as they conveniently
could, exercising as much bravery and honesty and
benevolence as they happened to possess, through a life
made up of unimportant tasks and tedious useless little
habits. Men felt the routine to be niggardly: but to-
morrow—and this was the sole point upon which their
priests and bonzes, their flamens and imauns, their
medicine men and popes and deacons, were unanimous,
—to-morrow would be quite different.

To-day alone was real. Never was a man brought into
contact with reality save through the evanescent emotions
and sensations of that single moment, that infinitesimal
fraction of a second, which was passing now,—and it was in
the insignificance of this moment, precisely, that pious
people must believe. So ran the teachings of all dead and
lingering faiths alike. Here was, perhaps, only another

instance of mankind's abhorrence of actualities; and man's quaint dislike of facing reality was here disguised as a high moral principle. That was why all art, which strove to make the sensations of a moment soul-satisfying, was dimly felt to be irreligious. For art performed what religion only promised.

CHAPTER **27**

Evolution of a Vestryman

BUT, much as man's religion looked to a more ordered and symmetrical existence to-morrow, just so, upon another scale, man's daily life seemed a continuous looking-forward to a terrestrial to-morrow. Kennaston could find in the past—even he, who was privileged to view the past in its actuality, rather than through the distorting media of books and national pride,—no suggestion as to what, if anything, he was expected to do while his physical life lasted, or to what, if anything, this life was a prelude. Yet that to-day was only a dull overture to to-morrow seemed in mankind an instinctive belief. All life everywhere, as all people spent it, was in preparation for something that was to happen to-morrow. This was as true of Antioch as Lichfield, as much the case with Charlemagne and Moses and Sardanapalus, and with Agamemnon and with Tiglath-Pileser, as with Felix Kennaston.

Kennaston considered his own life. . . . In childhood you had looked forward to being a man—a trapper of the plains or a railway engineer or a pirate, for choice, but, pending that, to get through the necessity of going to school five times a week. In vacations, of course, you looked forward to school's beginning again, because next term was to be quite different from the last, and moreover because last session, in retrospection, did not appear to have been half bad. And of course you were always wishing it would hurry up and be your birthday, or Christmas, or even Easter. . . .

Later, with puberty, had come the desire to be a devil with the women, like the fellows in Wycherley's plays (a cherished volume, which your schoolmates, unaccountably, did not find sufficiently "spicy"); and to become a great author, like Shakespeare; and to have plenty of money, like the Count of Monte-Cristo; and to be thrown with, and into the intimate confidence of, famous people, like the hero of a Scott novel. . . . Kennaston reflected that his touchstones seemed universally to have come from the library. . . . And Felix Kennaston had achieved his desire, to every intent, howsoever unapt was posterity to bracket him with Casanova or Don Juan, and howsoever many tourists still went with reverence to Stratford-upon-Avon rather than to Alcluid. He had enough money now to make taxes an ever-present nuisance; and quite certainly he had met more celebrities than any other person living.

Felix Kennaston reflected that, through accident's signal favor, he had done all he had at any time very earnestly wanted to do; and that the result was always disappointing, and not as it was depicted in story-books. . . . He wondered why he should again be harking back to literary standards.

Then it occurred to him that, in reality, he had always been shuffling through to-day—somehow and anyhow,—in the belief that to-morrow the life of Felix Kennaston would be converted into a romance like those in the story-books.

The transfiguring touch was to come, it seemed, from a girl's lips; but it had not; he kissed, and life remained uncharmed. It was to come from marriage, after which everything would be quite different; but the main innovation was that he missed the long delightful talks he used to have with Kathleen (mostly about Felix Kennaston), since as married people they appeared only to speak to each other, in passing, as it were, between the discharge of various domestic and social duties, and to speak then of having seen So-and-so, and of So-and-so's having said this-or-that. The transfiguring touch was to come from wealth; and it had not, for all that his address was in the *Social Register*, and was neatly typed in at the beginning of one copy of pretty much every appeal sent broadcast by charitable organizations. It

was to come from fame; and it had not, even with the nine
days' wonder over *Men Who Loved Alison*, and with Felix
Kennaston's pictorial misrepresentation figuring in public
journals, almost as prodigally as if he had murdered his wife
with peculiar brutality or headed a company to sell
inexpensive shoes. And, at the bottom of his heart, he was
still expecting the transfiguring touch to come, some day,
from something he was to obtain or do, perhaps to-morrow.
. . . Then he had by accident found out the sigil's power. . . .

Men everywhere were living as he had lived. People got
their notions of life, if only at second- or third-hand, from
books, precisely as he had done. Even Amrou had derived
his disastrous notions, as to the unimportance of books, from
a book. Men pretended laboriously that their own lives
were like the purposeful and clearly motived life of
book-land. In secret, the more perspicacious cherished the
reflection that, anyhow, their lives would begin to be like
that to-morrow. The purblind majority quite honestly
believed that literature was meant to mimic human life, and
that it did so. And in consequence, their love-affairs, their
maxims, their passions, their ethics, their conversations,
their so-called natural ties and instincts, and above all, their
wickednesses, became just so many bungling plagiarisms
from something they had read, in a novel or a Bible or a
poem or a newspaper.

People progressed from the kindergarten to the cemetery
assuming that their emotion at every crisis was what books
taught them was the appropriate emotion, and without
noticing that it was in reality something quite different.
Human life was a distorting, tarnished mirror held up to
literature: this much at least of Wilde's old paradox—that
life mimicked art,—was indisputable. Human life, very
clumsily, tried to reproduce the printed word. Human life
was prompted by, and was based upon, printed words,—"in
the beginning was the Word," precisely as Gospel asserted.

Kennaston had it now. Living might become symmetrical,
well-plotted, coherent and as rational as living was in books.
This was the hope which guided human beings through
to-day with anticipation of tomorrow.

Then he perceived that there was no such thing as
symmetry anywhere in inanimate nature. . . .

It was Ettarre who first pointed out to him the fact, so tremendously apparent when once observed, that there was to be found nowhere in inanimate nature any approach to symmetry. It needed only a glance toward the sky, after the falling of any reasonably clear night, to show there was no pattern-work in the arrangement of the stars. Nor were the planets moving about the sun at speeds or distances which bore any conceivable relation to one another. It was all at loose ends. He wondered how he could possibly have been misled by pulpit platitudes into likening this circumambient anarchy to mechanism. The universe showed on a sudden as a vast disheveled horror. There was no harmony, and no sense of order back of all this infinite torrent of gyrations. Interstellar space seemed to be just a jumble of frozen or flaming spheres that, moving ceaselessly, appeared to avoid one another's orbits, or to collide, by pure chance. This spate of stars, as in three monstrous freshets, might roughly serve some purpose; but there was to be found no more formal order therein than in the flow of water-drops over a mill-wheel.

And on earth there was no balancing in the distribution of land and water. Continents approached no regular shape. Mountains stood out like pimples or lay like broken welts across the habitable ground, with no symmetry of arrangement. Rivers ran anywhither, just as the haphazard slope of earth's crevices directed; upon the map you saw quite clearly that these streams neither balanced one another nor watered the land with any pretense of equity. There was no symmetry anywhere in inanimate nature, no harmony, no equipoise of parts, no sense of form, not even a straight line. It was all at loose ends, except—bewilderingly—when water froze. For then, as the microscope showed you, the ice-crystals were arranged in perfect and very elaborate patterns. And these stellular patterns, to the mused judgment of Kennaston, appeared to have been shaped by the last love-tap of unreason,—when, in completing all, unreason made sure that even here the universe should run askew to any conceivable "design" and lose even the coherency of being everywhere irregular.

But living things aimed toward symmetry. In plants the

notion seemed rudimentary, yet the goal was recognizable. The branches of a tree did not put out at ordered distance, nor could you discern any definite plan in their shaping: but in the leaves, at least, you detected an effort toward true balance: the two halves of a leaf, in a rough fashion, were equal. In every leaf and flower and grass-blade you saw this never entirely successful effort.

And in insects and reptiles and fish and birds and animals you saw again this effort, more creditably performed. All life seemed about the rather childish employment of producing a creature which consisted of two equal and exactly corresponding parts. It was true that in most cases this effort was foiled by an uneven distribution of color in plumage or scales or hide; but in insects and in mankind the goal, so far as went the eye, was reached. Men and insects, to the eye at least, could be divided into two equal halves. . . .

But even so, there was no real symmetry in man's body save in externals. The heart was not in the center, and the stomach appeared a sadly lopsided affair; there was no order in the jumbled viscera: all the internal organs of the human body seemed to have been thrust in as promiscuously as though this bag of flesh were a hand-bag packed at train-time in wild haste. Then, also, the two divisions of the brain did not correspond; there was nothing whatever on the left side to balance the troublesome vermiform appendix on the right; even the lines in the palm of one hand were unlike those which marked the other: and everywhere, in fine, there was some irrational discrepancy. Man, the highest form as yet of life, had attained at most only a teasing semblance of that crude symmetry toward which all life seemed to aim, and which inanimate nature appeared to ignore.

Nowhere in the universe could Kennaston discover any instance of quite equal balance, of anything which, as vision went, could be divided into two similar halves,—save only in man's handiwork. Here, again, insects approached man's efforts more closely than did the rest of creation; for many of them builded almost as truly. But man, alone in the universe, could produce exact visual symmetry, in a cathedral or a dinner-table or a pair of scissors, just as man so curiously mimicked symmetry in his outward appearance. The circumstance was droll, and no less quaint for the fact that it was quite probably without any significance. . . .

But Kennaston bemused himself with following out the notion that life was trying to evolve symmetry,—order, proportion and true balance. Living creatures represented life's gropings toward that goal. You saw, no doubt, a dim perception of this in the dream which sustained all human beings,—that to-morrow living would begin to be symmetrical, well plotted, and coherent, like the progress of a novel. . . . And that was precisely what religion promised, only in more explicit terms, and with the story's milieu fixed in romantic, rather than realistic, settings.

Kennaston had here the sensation of fitting in the last bit of a puzzle. Life, yearning for symmetry, stood revealed as artist. Life strove toward the creation of art. That was all life cared about. Living things were more or less successful works of art, and were to be judged according to art's canons alone. The universe was life's big barren studio, which the artist, certainly, had neither planned nor builded, but had, somehow, occupied, to make the best of its limitations. For Kennaston insisted that living things and inanimate nature had none of the earmarks of being by the same author. They were not in similar style, he said; thus, presupposing a sentient creator of the stars and planets, it would seem to have been in contradiction of his code to make both of a man's eyes the same color.

It was this course of speculation which converted Kennaston to an abiding faith in Christianity, such as, our rector informs me, is deplorably rare in these lax, pleasure-loving days of materialism.

To believe this inconsiderable planet the peculiar center of a God's efforts and attention had for a long while strained Kennaston's credulity: the thing was so woefully out of proportion when you considered earth's relative value in the universe. But now Felix Kennaston comprehended that in the insensate universe there was no proportion. The idea was unknown to the astral architect, or, at best, no part of his plan, if indeed there had been any premeditation or contriver concerned.

Singly on our small earth—and nowhere else, so far as man might judge, not even in the solar system of which earth made a part,—was any sense of proportion evinced; and upon earth this sense of proportion was apparent only in living things. Kennaston now seemed to glimpse an Artist-God, with a commendable sense of form, —Kennaston's fellow craftsman,—and the planet earth as that corner of the studio wherein the God was working, at present, and all life as a romance which the God was inditing. . . .

That the plot of this romance began with Eden and reached its climax at Calvary, Kennaston was persuaded, solely and ardently, because of the surpassing beauty of the Christ-legend. No other myth compared with it from an aesthetic standpoint. He could imagine no theme more adequate to sustain a great romance than this of an Author suffering willingly for His puppets' welfare; and mingling with His puppets in the similitude of one of them; and able to wring only contempt and pity from His puppets,—since He had not endowed them with any faculties wherewith to comprehend their Creator's nature and intent.

Indeed, it was pretty much the plight which Kennaston had invented for his own puppets at Storisende, as Kennaston complacently reflected. It was the most tremendous "situation" imaginable; and quite certainly no Author could ever have failed to perceive, and to avail Himself of, its dramatic possibilities. To conceive that the world-romance did not center upon Calvary was to presume an intelligent and skilled Romancer blind to the basic principles of His art. His sense of pathos and of beauty and of irony could have led Him to select no other legend. And in the inconsistencies and unsolved problems, or even the apparent contradictions, of Christianity, Felix Kennaston could see only a possible error or omission on the Author's part, such as was common to all romances. A few errata did not hamper the tale's worth and splendor, or render it a whit less meritorious of admiration. . . .

And, by and by, Felix Kennaston found that his theory of the Atonement was in harmony with quite orthodox teachings. The library at Alcluid revealed bewildered and perturbed generations at guess-work. How could a God have been placated, and turned from wrath and benevolence, by witnessing the torment of His own son? What pleasure, whereby He was propitiated, could the God have derived from watching the scene on Calvary? Or was the God, as priests had taught so long (within the same moment that they proclaimed the God's omnipotence), not wholly a free agent, because bound by laws whereby He was compelled to punish someone for humanity's disobedience, with the staggering option of substituting an innocent victim? For if you granted that, you conceded to be higher than the God, and overruling Him, a power which made for flat injustice.

Since Schleiermacher's time, at least, as Kennaston discovered, there had been reasoning creatures to contest the possibility of such discrepant assumptions, and a dynasty of teachers who adhered to the "subjective" theory of propitiation. For these considered that Christ came, not primarily to be crucified, but by his life to reveal to men the nature of their God. The crucifixion was an incidental and almost inevitable result of human obtuseness; and all the regrettable events of our first Good Friday were of value only in that through them the full extent of divine love was perfectly evinced. The personality, rather than the sufferings, of the Nazarene had thus satisfied, not any demand or attribute of the God by acting upon it from without, "but God's total nature by revealing it and realizing it in humanity." The God, in short, had satisfied Himself "by revealing and expressing His nature" in the material universe, precisely as lesser artists got relief from the worries of existence by depicting themselves in their books.

Just as poets express themselves communicatively in words, so here the Author had expressed Himself in flesh. Such, in effect, had been the teaching of Karl Immanuel Nitzsch, of Richard Rothe, and of Von Hofman, in Germany; of Auguste Bouvier in Geneva; of Alexandre Vinet, and of Auguste Sabatier, in France; of Frederick Denison Maurice, and John Caird, and Benjamin Jowett, in England; and, in America, of Horace Bushnell, and Elisha Mulford, and William Newton Clarke. The list was imposing; and Kennaston rejoiced to find himself at one with so many reputable theologians. For all these scholars had dimly divined, with whatsoever variousness they worded the belief, that the God's self-satisfaction sprang from the consciousness of having, at last, done a really fine piece of artistic work, in creating the character of Christ. . . .

So, as nearly as one can phrase the matter, it was as an expression of entire confidence in his Author's literary abilities that Felix Kennaston was now confirmed, at our little country church, to the delight of his wife and the approbation of his neighbors. It was felt to be eminently suitable: that such a quiet, well-to-do man of his years and station should not be a communicant was generally, indeed, adjudged unnatural. And when William T. Vartrey (of the Lichfield Iron Works) was gathered to his grandfathers, in the following autumn, Mr. Kennaston was rather as a matter of course elected to succeed him in the vestry. And Kennaston was unfeignedly pleased and flattered.

To the discerning it is easy enough to detect, in all this fantastic theorizing, the man's obsessing love of ordered beauty and his abhorrence of slovenliness and shapelessness—very easy to see just what makes the writings of Felix Kennaston most admirable,—here alluring him to believe that such ideals must also be cherished by Omnipotence. This poet loved his formal art to the extent of coming to assume it was the purpose and the origin of terrestrial life. Life seemed to him, in short, a God's chosen form of artistic self-expression; and as a confrère, Kennaston found the result praiseworthy. Even inanimate nature, he sometimes thought, might be a divine experiment in *vers libre*. . . . But neither the justice of Kennaston's airdrawn surmises, nor their wildness, matters; the point is that they made of him a vestryman who in appearance and speech and actions, and in essential beliefs, differed not at all from his associates in office, who had comfortably acquired their standards by hearsay. It follows that the moral of his theorizing should be no less obvious than salutary.

CHAPTER **28**

The Shallowest Sort of Mysticism

THROUGH such airdrawn surmises, then, as I have just recorded did Felix Kennaston enter at last into that belief which is man's noblest heritage. . . .

"Or I would put it, rather, that belief is man's métier," Kennaston once corrected me,—"for the sufficient reason that man has nothing to do with certainties. He cannot ever get in direct touch with reality. Such is the immutable law, the true cream of the jest. Felix Kennaston, so long as he wears the fleshly body of Felix Kennaston, is conscious only of various tiny disturbances in his brain-cells, which entertain and interest him, but cannot pretend to probe to the roots of reality about anything. By the nature of my mental organs, it is the sensation the thing arouses in my brain of which I am aware, and never of the thing itself. I am conscious only of appearances. They may all be illusory. I cannot ever tell. But it is my human privilege to believe whatever I may elect."

"Yet, my dear sir," as I pointed out, "is not this hair-splitting, really, a reduction of human life to the very shallowest sort of mysticism, that gets you nowhere?"

"Now again, Harrowby, you are falling into the inveterate race-delusion that man is intended to get somewhere. I do not see that the notion rests on any readily apparent basis. It is, at any rate, a working hypothesis that in the world-romance man, being cast for the part of fool, quite obviously best furthers the dénouement's success by wearing his motley bravely. . . . There was a fool in my own romance, you may remember, a character of no great importance; yet it was an essential incident in the story that he should irresponsibly mislay the King's letter, and that Sir Guiron should thus be forced to seek service under Duke Florestan.

Perhaps, in similar fashion, it is here necessary to the Author's scheme that man must simply go on striving to gain a little money, food, and sleep, a trinket or two, some moments of laughter, and at the last, a decent bed to die in. It very well may be that man's allotted part calls for just these actions, to round out the drama artistically. Yes; it is quite conceivable that, much as I shaped events at Storisende, so here the Author aims toward making an aesthetic masterpiece of His puppet-play as a whole, rather than at ending everything with a transformation scene such as, when we were younger, used so satisfactorily to close *The Black Crook* and *The Devil's Auction*. For it may well be that the Author has, after all, more in common with Aeschylus, say, than with the Charles H. Yale who catered to our boyhood with those spectacular diversions. . . . So I must train my mind to be contented with appearances, whether they be true or not,—reserving always a permissible preference for the illusion which seems the more pleasant. Being mortal, I am able to contrive no thriftier bargain."

"Being mortal," I amended, "we pick our recreations to suit our tastes. Now I, for instance—as is, indeed, a matter of some notoriety and derision here in Lichfield,—am interested in what people loosely speak of as 'the occult.'. . . No, I do not attempt to persuade defunct poetesses to dictate, via the Ouija board, effusions which give little encouragement as to the present state of culture in Paradise, or to induce Napoleon to leave wherever he is and devote his energies to tipping a table about the room for my entertainment. That sort of thing is tosh. . . . Yet I fixedly believe the Wardens of Earth sometimes unbar strange windows, that face on other worlds than ours. And some of us, I think, once in a while get a peep through these windows. But we are not permitted to get a long peep, or an unobstructed peep, nor, very certainly, are we permitted to see all there is—out yonder. The fatal fault, sir, of your theorizing is that it is too complete. It aims to throw light upon the universe, and therefore is self-evidently moonshine. The Wardens of Earth do not desire that we should understand the universe, Mr. Kennaston; it is part of Their appointed task to ensure that we never do; and because of Their efficiency every notion that any man, dead, living, or unborn, might form as to the universe will necessarily prove wrong. So, if for no other reason, I must decline to think of you and me as characters in a romance."

PART FIVE

**Which follows after Ettarre and
wins to every poet's reward**

"This was the measure of my soul's delight;
It had no power of joy to fly by day,
Nor part in the large lordship of the light;
But in a secret moon-beholden way
Had all its will of dreams and pleasant night,
And all the love and life that sleepers may.

"But such life's triumphs as men waking may
It might not have to feed its faint delight."

CHAPTER 29

Of Poetic Love: Treated with Poetic Inefficiency

SO much for what Kennaston termed his "serious reading" in chance-opened pages of the past. There were other dreams quite different in nature, which seemed, rather, to fulfil the function of romantic art, in satisfying his human craving for a full-fed emotional existence,—dreams which Kennaston jestingly described as "belles lettres." For now by turn—as murderer, saint, herdsman, serf, fop, pickpurse, troubadour, monk, bravo, lordling, monarch, and in countless other estates,—Kennaston tasted those fruitless emotions which it is the privilege of art to arouse, and gained large-hearted joys without any inevitable purchase-price, and regrets that were not bitter, and miseries which left him not a penny the worse.

But it was as a lover that his rôle quite engrossed him, in many dreams wherein he bore for Ettarre such adoration as he had always wistfully hoped he might entertain toward some woman some day, and had not ever known in his waking hours. It was sober truth he had spoken at Storisende: "There is no woman like you in my country, Ettarre. I can find no woman anywhere resembling you whom dreams alone may win to." But now at last, even though it were only in dreams, he loved as he had always dimly felt he was capable of loving. . . . Even the old lost faculty of verse-making seemed to come back to him with this change, and he began again to fashion rhymes, elaborating bright odd vignettes of foiled love in out-of-the-way epochs and surroundings. These were the verses included, later, under the general title of "Dramatis Personae," in his *Chimes at Midnight*.

He wrote of foiled love necessarily, since not even as a lover might he win to success. It was the cream of some supernal jest that he might not touch Ettarre; that done, though but by accident, the dream ended, and the universe seemed to fold about him, just as a hand closes. He came to understand the reason of this. "Love must look toward something not quite accessible, something not quite understood," he had said at Storisende: and this phrase, so lightly despatched, came home to him now as pregnant truth. For it was this fact which enabled him to love Ettarre, and had always prevented his loving any other woman.

All mortal women either loved some other man, and went with him somewhither beyond the area of your daily life, and so, in time were forgotten; or, else, they loved you, and laid bare to you their minds and bodies,—and neither of these possessions ever proved so remarkable, when calmly viewed, as to justify any continued infatuation therewith. Such at least Felix Kennaston had always found to be the case: love did not live, as lovers do, by feeding; but, paradoxically, got strength by hungering. It should be remembered, however, that Felix Kennaston was a poet. . . .

He would sometimes think of the women who had loved him; and would speculate, with some wistfulness, if it was invariably true, as with his own amorous traffic, that love both kept and left its victims strangers to each other? He knew so little of these soft-lipped girls and women, when everything was said. . . .

Yet there had been—he counted,—yes, time had known eight chaste and comely gentlewomen, in all, who had "given themselves to him," as the hackneyed phrase was. These eight affairs, at any event, had conformed to every tradition, and had been as thorough-going as might romantically be expected: but nothing much seemed to have come of them; and he did not feel in the upshot very well acquainted with their heroines. His sole emotion toward them nowadays was that of mild dislike. But six of them—again to utilize a venerable conjunction of words,—had "deceived their husbands" for the caresses of an impecunious Kennaston; and the other two had anticipatorily "deceived" the husbands they took later: so that they must, he reflected, have loved Felix Kennaston sincerely.

He was quite certain, though, that he had never loved any one of them as he had always wanted to love. No one of these women had given him what he sought in vain. Kennaston had felt this lack of success dispiritedly when, with soft arms about him, it was necessary to think of what he would say next. He had always in such circumstances managed to feign high rapture, to his temporary companion's entire satisfaction, as he believed; but each adventure left him disappointed. It had not roused in him the overwhelming emotions which lovers had in books, nor anything resembling these emotions; and that was what he had wanted, and had not ever realized, until the coming of Ettarre. . . .

He had made love, as a prevalent rule, to married women,—allured, again, by bookish standards, which advanced the commerce of Lancelot with Guenevere, or of Paolo Malatesta with his brother's wife, as the supreme type of romantic passion. On more practical grounds, Kennaston preferred married women, partly because they were less stupid to converse with in general, and in particular did not bring up the question of marrying you; and in part because the husband in the background helped the situation pictorially,—this notion also now seemed to be of literary origin, —besides furnishing an unfailing topic of conversation.

For unfaithful or wavering wives, to Kennaston's finding, peculiarly delighted in talking about their husbands; and in such prattle failed either to exhibit the conventional remorse toward, or any very grave complaint against, the discussed better-half. The inconsistency would have worried Kennaston's sense of justice, had not these husbands always been so unconcealedly certain of Kennaston's insignificance. . . . Although judging of necessity only from his own experience, Kennaston was unable conscientiously to approve of adulterous love-affairs: they tended too soon toward tediousness; and married women seemed horribly quick to become matter-of-fact in the details of a liaison, and ready almost to confuse you with the husband.

The giggle and chatter of young girls Kennaston had always esteemed unalluring, even in his own youth. He had admired a number of them extravagantly, but only as ornamental objects upon which very ill-advisedly had been conferred the gift of speech. To-day he looked back wistfully at times, as we must all do, to that girl who first had asked him if he was sure that he respected her as much as ever: but it was with the mental annotation that she had seven children now, and, as Kathleen put it, not a ray of good looks left.

And he would meditate that he had certainly been fond of Margaret Hugonin, even though in the beginning it was her money which attracted him; and that Marian Winwood, despite her underhanded vengeance in publishing his letters, had been the most delectable of company all that ancient summer when it had rained so persistently. Then there had been tall Ida Vartrey, like a statue of gold and ivory; Kitty Provis, with those wonderful huge green eyes of hers; and Celia Reindan, she who wore that curious silver band across her forehead; and Helen Strong; and Blanche Druro; and Muriel. . . .

In memory they arose like colorful and gracious phantoms, far more adorable than they had ever been on earth, when each of these had loaned, for a season, the touch of irresolute soft hands and friendly lips to a half-forgotten Felix Kennaston. All these, and others, had been, a long while since, the loveliest creatures that wore tender human flesh: and so, they had kissed, and they had talked time-hallowed nonsense, and they had shed the orthodox tears; and—also a long while since,—they had died or they had married the conventional someone else: and it did not matter the beard of an onion to the pudgy pasty man that Felix Kennaston had come to be. He had possessed, or else of his own volition he had refrained from possessing, all these brightly-colored moth-brained girls: but he had loved none of them as he had always known he was capable of loving: and at best, these girls were dead now, or at worst, they had been converted into unaccountable people. . . .

Kathleen was returning from the South that day, and Kennaston had gone into Lichfield to meet her train. The Florida Express was late by a full hour; so he sat in their motor-car, waiting, turning over some verses in his torpid mind, and just half-noticing persons who were gathering on the station platform to take the noon train going west. He was reflecting how ugly and how trivial the faces of mankind appear when any crowd is viewed collectively, —and he was wondering if the Author, looking down into a hot thronged street, was never tempted to obliterate the human race as an unsuccessful experiment,—when Kennaston recognized Muriel Allardyce.

"I simply will not see her," he decided.

He turned his back that way, picked up the morning paper on the seat beside him, and began to read an editorial on immigration. What the deuce was she doing in Lichfield, any way? She lived in St. Louis now. She was probably visiting Avis Blagden. Evidently, she was going west on the noon train. If Kathleen's train arrived before midday he would have to get out of the car to meet her, and all three would come together on the platform. If Muriel spied him there, in the open car, it would be not uncharacteristic of her to join him. And he could not go away, because Kathleen's train was apt to arrive any minute. It was perfectly damnable. Why could the woman not stay in St. Louis, where she belonged, instead of gadding about the country? Thus Kennaston, as he reread the statistics as to Poles and Magyars.

"I think there's two ladies trying to speak to you, sir," the chauffeur hazarded.

"Eh?—oh, yes!" said Kennaston.

He looked, perforce, and saw that across the railway track both Muriel Allardyce and Avis Blagden were regarding him with idiotic grins and wavings. He lifted his hat, smiled, waved his own hand, and retired between the pages of the *Lichfield Courier-Herald*. Muriel was wearing a light traveling veil, he reflected; he could pretend not to know who she was. With recognition, of course, he would be expected to come over and speak to her. He must remember to ask Avis, the very next time he saw her, who had been that familiar-looking person with her, and to express regret for his short-sightedness. . . .

He decided to step out of the car, by way of the farther door, and buy a package of cigarettes on the other side of the street. He could loaf there and pray that Muriel's train might leave before Kathleen's train had arrived. . . .

"I don't believe you recognized us," said Avis Blagden, at his elbow. "Or else you are trying to cut your old playmates."

The two women had brazenly pursued him. They were within a yard of him. It was indelicate. It was so perfectly unnecessary. He cordially wished some friendly engine had run them both down when they were crossing the tracks. . . .

"Why, bless my soul!" he was saying, "this is indeed a delightful surprise. I had no idea you were in town, Mrs. Allardyce. I didn't recognize you, with that veil on—"

"There's Peter at last," said Avis. "I really must speak to him a moment."

And she promptly left them. Kennaston reflected that the whole transaction was self-evidently prearranged. And Muriel was, as if abstractedly, but deliberately, walking beyond earshot of the chauffeur. And there was nothing for it save to accompany her.

"It's awfully jolly to see you again," he observed, with fervor.

"Is it? Honestly, Felix, it looked almost as if you were trying to avoid me." Kennaston wondered how he could ever have loved a woman of so little penetration.

"No, I didn't recognize you, with that veil on," he repeated. "And I had no idea you were in Lichfield. I do hope you are going to pay us all a nice long visit—"

"But, no, I am leaving on this train—"

"Oh, I say, but that's too bad! And I never knew you were here!" he lamented.

"I only stopped overnight with Avis. I am on my way home—"

"To Leonard?" And Kennaston smiled. "How do you get on with him nowadays?"

"We are—contented, I suppose. He has his business—and politics. He is doing perfectly splendidly now, you know. And I have my memories." Her voice changed. "I have my memories, Felix! Nothing—nothing can take that from me!"

"Good God, Muriel, there are a dozen people watching us—"

"What does that matter!"

"Well, it matters a lot to me. I live here, you know."

She was silent for a moment. "You look your latest rôle in life so well, too, Felix. You are the respectable married gentleman to the last detail. Why, you are an old man now, Felix," she said wistfully. "Your hair is gray about the ears, and you are fat, and there are wrinkles under your eyes—But are you happy, dear?" she asked, with the grave tender speech that he remembered. And momentarily the man forgot the people about them, and the fact that his wife's train was due any minute.

"Happier than I deserve to be, Muriel." His voice had quavered,—had quavered in fact very nicely, it appeared to him.

"That's true, at least," the woman said, as in reflection. "You treated me rather abominably, you know,—like an old shoe."

"I am not altogether sorry you take that view of it. For I wouldn't want you to regret—anything,—not even that which, to me at least, is very sacred. But there was really nothing else to do save just to let things end. It was as hard," he said, with a continuous flight of imagination, "it was as hard on me as you."

"Sometimes I think it was simply because you were afraid of Leonard. I put that out of my mind, though, always. You see, I like to keep my memories. I have nothing else now, Felix—" She opened the small leather bag she carried, took out a handkerchief, and brushed her lips. "I am a fool, of course. Oh, it is funny to see your ugly little snub nose again! And I couldn't help wanting to speak to you, once more—"

"It has been delightful. And some day I certainly do hope—But there's your train, I think. The gates are going down."

"And here is Avis coming. So good-by, Felix. It is really forever this time, I think—"

It seemed to him that she held in her left hand the sigil of Scoteia. . . . He stared at the gleaming thing, then raised his eyes to hers. She was smiling. Her eyes were the eyes of Ettarre. All the beauty of the world seemed gathered in this woman's face. . . .

"Don't let it be forever! Come with me, Felix! There is only you—even now, there is only you. It is not yet too late—" Astounding as were the words, they came quite clearly, in a pleading, frightened half-whisper.

The man was young for just that one wonderful moment of inexplicable yearning and self-loathing. Then, "I am afraid my wife would hardly like it," he said, equably. "So good-by, Muriel. It has been very delightful to see you again."

"I was mistaken, though, of course. It was the top of a vanity-box, or of a toilet-water flask, or of something else, that she took out of the bag, when she was looking for her handkerchief. It was just a silly coincidence. I was mistaken, of course. . . . And here is Kathleen's train. Thank goodness, it was late enough. . . ."

Thus Kennaston, as he went to receive his wife's cool kiss. And—having carefully mentioned, as a matter of no earthly importance, that he had just seen Muriel Allardyce, and that she had gone off terribly in looks, and that none of them seem to hold their own like you, dear,—he debarred from mind that awkward moment's delusion, and tried not to think of it any more.

CHAPTER **30**

Cross-Purposes in Spacious Times

SO KENNASTON SEEMED to have got only disappointment and vexation and gainless vague regret from his love-affairs in the flesh; and all fleshly passion seemed to flicker out inevitably, howsoever splendid the brief blaze. For you loved and lost; or else you loved and won: there was quick ending either way. And afterward unaccountable women haunted you, and worried you into unreasonable contrition, in defiance of common-sense. . . .

But for Ettarre, who embodied all Kennaston was ever able to conceive of beauty and fearlessness and strange purity, all perfections, all the attributes of divinity, in a word, such as his slender human faculties were competent to understand, he must hunger always in vain. Whatever happened, Ettarre stayed inaccessible, even in dreams: her beauty was his to look on only; and always when he came too near that radiant loveliness which was Ettarre's—that perfect beauty which was so full of troubling reticences, and so, was touched with something sinister,—then the dream would end, and the universe would seem to fold about him, just as a hand closes. Such was the law, the kindly law, as Kennaston now believed, through which love might thrive even in the arid heart of a poet.

Sometimes, however, this law would lead to odd results, and left the dream an enigma. For instance, he had a quaint experience upon the night of that day during which he had talked with Muriel Allardyce. . . .

"You are in all things a fortunate man, Master—ah —whatever your true name may be," said the boy, pettishly flinging down the cards.

"Ods life, and have we done?" says Kennaston. . . .

The two sat in a comfortable paneled room. There was a big open fire behind Kennaston; he could see its reflections flicker about the woodwork. The boy facing him was glowingly attired in green and gold, an ardent comely urchin, who (as Kennaston estimated) might perhaps be a page to Queen Elizabeth, or possibly was one of King James's spoilt striplings. Between them was a rough deal table, littered with playing-cards; and upon it sat a tallish blue pitcher half-full of wine, four lighted candles stuck like corks in as many emptied bottles, and two coarse yellow mugs. . . .

"Yes, we have done," the boy answered; and, rising, smiled cherubically. "May I ask what is the object that you conceal with such care in your left hand?"

"To be candid," Kennaston returned, "it is the King of Diamonds, that swarthy bearded Spaniard. I had intended it

should serve as a corrective and encourager of Lady
Fortune, when I turned it, my next deal, as the trump card.
I'faith, I thank God I have found the jade is to be
influenced by such small hints. Oh, ay, sir, I may say it
without conceit that my fingers have in these matters some
tolerable compass and variety."

"A card-sharp!" sneers the boy. "La, half of us suspected
it already; but it will be rare news to the town that Master
Lionel Branch—as I must continue to call you,—stands
detected in such Greek knaveries."

"Nay," Kennaston answered, "but you will hardly live to
moralize of it, sir. Oh, no, sir, indeed my poor arts must not
be made public: for I would not seem to boast of my
accomplishments. Harkee, sir, I abhor vainglory. I name no
man, sir; but I know very well there are snotty-nosed
people who accord to these expedients for amending the
quirks of fate their starched disfavor. Hah, but, signior, what
is that to us knights of the moon, to us gallants of more
generous spirit?—Oh, Lord, sir, I protest I look upon such
talents much as I do upon my breeches and my codpiece. I
do consider them as possessions, not certainly to be
vaunted, but indispensable to any gentleman who hopes to
make a pleasing figure in the world's eye."

The boy said: "All this bluster is wordy foolery, Master
Branch. What I have seen, I have seen; and you will readily
guess how I mean to use my knowledge."

"I would give a great deal to find out what he is talking
about," was Kennaston's reflection. "I have discovered, at
least, that my present alias is Branch, but that I am in reality
somebody else." Aloud he said: " 'Fore God, your eyesight
is of the best, Master Skirlaw—(*How the deuce did I know
his name, now?*)—Hah, I trust forthwith to prove if your
sword be equally keen."

The boy replied, "I will fight with no cheats—"

"I'faith, sir," Kennaston cried out gaily, "but I have heard
that wine is a famed provoker of courage. Let us try the
byword."

So saying, Kennaston picked up one mug, and flung its
contents full in the boy's face. It was white wine, Kennaston

noted, for it did not stain Master Skirlaw's handsome countenance at all.

"The insult is sufficient. Draw, and have done!" the lad said quietly. His sword gleamed in the restive reflections of that unseen fire behind Kennaston.

"Na, na! but, my most expeditious cockerel," Kennaston replied, "this place is a thought too public. Now yonder is a noble courtyard. Oh, ay, favored by to-night's moon, we may settle our matter without any hindrance or intolerable scandal. So, I will call my host, that we may have the key. Yet, upon my gentility, Master Skirlaw, I greatly fear I shall be forced to kill you. Therefore I cry you mercy, sir, but is there on your mind no business which you would not willingly leave undischarged? Save you, friend, but we are all mortal. Hah, to a lady whom I need not name, it is an affair of considerable import what disposition a bold man might make of this ring—"

Leering, Kennaston touched the great signet-ring on the lad's thumb; and forthwith the universe seemed to fold about him, just as a hand closes. In this brief moment of inexplicable yearning and self-loathing he comprehended that the boy's face was the face of Ettarre.

And Kennaston, awake, was pleading, with meaningless words, "Valentia! forgive me, Valentia! . . . ."

And that was all. This dream remained an enigma. Kennaston could never know what events had preceded this equivocal instant, or how Ettarre came to be disguised as a boy, or what were their relations in this dream, nor, above all, why he should have awakened crying upon the name of Valentia. It was simply a law that always when he was about to touch Ettarre—even unconsciously,—everything must vanish; and through the workings of that law this dream, with many others, came to be just a treasured moment of unexplainable but poignant emotion.

CHAPTER **31**

Horvendile to Ettarre:
At Whitehall

TO KENNASTON the Lord Protector was saying, with grave unction: "You will, I doubt not, fittingly express to our friends in Virginia, Master Major, those hearty sentiments which I have in the way of gratefulness, in that I have received the honor and safeguard of their approbation; for all which I humbly thank them. To our unfriends in that colony we will let action speak when I shall have completed God's work in Ireland."

"Yet the Burgesses, sir, are mostly ill-affected," Kennaston found himself saying; "and Berkeley, to grant him justice, does not lack bravery—"

Cromwell replied: "With Heaven's help, Master Major, I have of late dealt with a king who did not lack bravery. Nay, depend upon it, I shall some day grant William Berkeley utter justice,—such justice as I gave his master, that proud curled man, Charles Stuart."

Then the Lord Protector's face was changed, and his harsh countenance became a little troubled. "Yes, I shall do all this, with Heaven's help, I think. But in good faith, I grow old, Master Major. I move in a mist, and my deeds are strange to me. . . ."

Cromwell closed and unclosed his hands, regarding them; and he sighed. Then it was to Ettarre he spoke:

"I leave you in Master Major's charge. It may be I shall not return alive into England; indeed, I grow an old man and feel infirmities of age stealing upon me. And so, farewell, my lass. Truly if I love you not too well, I err not on the other hand much. Thou hast been dearer to me than any other creature: let that suffice."

And with this leave-taking the Lord Protector was gone.

As the door closed upon Cromwell's burly figure, "No, be very careful not to touch me," Kennaston implored. "The dream must last till I have found out how through your aid, Ettarre, this bull-necked country squire has come to rule England. It is precisely as I expected. You explain Cromwell, you explain Mohammed,—Richelieu and Tamburlaine and Julius Caesar, I suspect, and, as I know, Napoleon,—all these men who have inexplicably risen from nothing to earthly supremacy. How is it done, Ettarre?"

"It is not I who contrive it, Horvendile. I am but an incident in such men's lives. They have known me—yes: and knowing me, they were bent enough on their own ends to forget that I seemed not unlovely. It is not the sigil and the power the sigil gives which they love and serve—"

"And that small square mirror, such as Cromwell also carried—?" Kennaston began. "Or is this forbidden talk?"

"Yes, that mirror aids them," Ettarre replied. "In that mirror they can see only themselves. So the mirror aids toward the ends they chose, with open eyes. . . . But you cannot ever penetrate these mysteries now, Horvendile. The secret of the mirror was offered you once, and you would not bargain. The secret of the mirror is offered to no man twice."

And Kennaston laughed merrily. "What does it matter? I am perfectly content. That is more than can be said for yonder sanctimonious fat old rascal, who has just told me he is going into Ireland 'for the propagating of the gospel of Christ, the establishing of truth and peace, and the restoring of that bleeding nation to its former happiness and tranquility.' Why is it that people of executive ability seem always to be more or less mentally deficient? Now, you and I know that, in point of fact, he is going into Ireland to burn villages, massacre women, hang bishops, and generally qualify his name for all time as a Hibernian synonym for infamy. Oh, no, the purchase-price of grandeur is too great; and men that crown themselves in this world inevitably perform the action with soiled hands. Still, I wish I had known I was going visiting to-night in seventeenth-century England," said Kennaston, reflectively; "then I could have read up a bit. I don't even know whether Virginia ever submitted to him. It simply shows what idleness may lead to! If I had studied history more faithfully I would have been able tonight to prophesy to Oliver Cromwell about the results of his Irish campaigns and so on, and could have impressed him vastly with my abilities. As it is, I have missed an opportunity which will probably not ever occur again to any man of my generation. . . ."

CHAPTER 32

Horvendile to Ettarre: At Vaux-le-Vicomte

WHAT FUN!" says Kennaston; "we are at Vaux-le-Vicomte, where Fouquet is entertaining young Louis Quatorze. Yonder is La Vallière,—the thin tow-headed girl, with the big mouth. People are just beginning to whisper scandal about her. And that tall jade is Athenaïs de Tonnay-Charente,—the woman who is going to be Madame de Montespan and control everything in the kingdom later on, you remember. The King is not yet aware of her existence, nor has Monsieur de Montespan been introduced. . . .

"The Troupe of Monsieur is about to present an open-air comedy. It is called *Les Facheux*,—The Bores. It is rumored to take off very cleverly the trivial tedious fashion in which perfectly well-meaning people chatter their way through life. But that more fittingly would be the theme of a tragedy, Ettarre. Men are condemned eternally to bore one another. Two hundred years and more from to-day—perhaps forever,—man will lack means, or courage, to voice his actual thoughts adequately. He must still talk of weather probabilities and of having seen So-and-so and of such trifles, that mean to him absolutely nothing,—and must babble of these things even to the persons who are most dear and familiar to him. Yes, every reputable man must desperately make small-talk, and echo and re-echo senseless phrases, until the crack of doom. He will always be afraid to bare his actual thoughts and interests to his fellow's possible disapproval: or perhaps it is just a pitiable mania with the race. At all events, one should not laugh at this ageless aspersion and burlesque of man's intelligence as performed by man himself. . . .

"The comedy is quite new. A marquis, with wonderful canions and a scented wig like an edifice, told me it is by an upholsterer named Coquelin, a barnstormer who ran away from home and has been knocking about the provinces unsuccessfully for nearly twenty years: and my little marquis wondered what in the world we are coming to, when Monsieur le Surintendent takes up with that class of people. Is not my little marquis droll?—for he meant Poquelin, soon to be Poquelin de Molière, of course. Molière, also, is a name which is not famous, as yet. But in a month or so it will be famous for all time; and Monsieur le Surintendent will be in jail and forgotten. . . .

"You smile, Ettarre? Ah, yes, I understand. Molière too adores you. All poets have had fitful glimpses of you, Ettarre, and of that perfect beauty which is full of troubling reticences, and so, is touched with something sinister. I have written as to the price they pay, these hapless poets, in a little book I am inditing through that fat pudgy body I wear in the flesh. . . . Do not frown: I know it is forbidden to talk with you concerning my life in the flesh. . . .

"Ah, the King comes,—evidently in no very amiable frame of mind,—and all rise, like a flurry of great butterflies. It is the beginning of the play. See, a woman is coming out of the big shell in the fountain. . . .

"I wish my old friend Jonas d'Artagnan were here. It is a real pity he is only a character in fiction,—just as I once thought you to be, Ettarre. Eh, what a fool I was to imagine I had created you! and that I controlled your speech and doings! I know much better now. . . .

"Ettarre, your unattainable beauty tears my heart. Is that black-browed Molière your lover too? What favors have you granted him? You perceive I am jealous. How can I be otherwise, when there is nothing, nothing in me, that does not cry out for love of you? And I am forbidden ever to win quite to you, ever to touch you, ever to see you even save in my dreams!"

CHAPTER **33**

Horvendile to Ettarre: In the Conciergerie

THEY WAITED in a big dark room of the Conciergerie, with many other condemned emigrants, until the tumbrils should come to fetch them to the Place de la Révolution. They stood beneath a narrow barred window, set high in the wall, so that thin winter sunlight made the girl's face visible. Misery was about them, death waited without: and it did not matter a pennyworth.

"Ettarre, I know to-day that all my life I have been seeking you. Very long ago when I was a child it was made clear that you awaited me somewhere; and, I recollect now, I used to hunger for your coming with a longing which has not any name. And when I went about the dusty world I still believed you waited somewhere,—till I should find you, as I inevitably must, or soon or late. Did I go upon a journey to some unfamiliar place?—it might be that unwittingly I traveled toward your home. I could never pass a walled garden where green tree-tops showed, without suspecting, even while I shrugged to think how wild was the imagining, that there was only the wall between us. I did not know the color of your eyes, but I knew what I would read there. And for a fevered season I appeared to encounter many women of earth who resembled you—"

"All women resemble me, Horvendile. Whatever flesh they may wear as a garment, and howsoever time-frayed or dull-hued or stained by horrible misuse that garment may seem to be, the wearer of that garment is no less fair than I, could any man see her quite clearly. Horvendile, were that not true, could our great Author find anywhere a woman's body which wickedness and ugliness controlled unchecked, all the big stars which light the universe, and even the tiny sun that our earth spins about, would be blown out like unneeded candles, for the Author's labor would have been frustrated and misspent."

"Yes; I know now that this is true. . . . See, Ettarre! Yonder woman is furtively coloring her cheeks with a little wet red rag. She does not wish to seem pale—or is it that she wishes to look her best?—in the moment of death. . . . Ettarre, my love for you whom I could not ever find, was not of earth, and I could not transfer it to any of our women. The lively hues, the lovely curvings and the fragrant tender flesh of earth's women were deft to cast their spells; but presently I knew this magic was only of the body. It might be I was honoring divinity; but it was certain that even in such case I was doing so by posturing before my divinity's effigy in tinted clay. Besides, it is not possible to know with any certainty what is going on in the round glossy little heads of women. 'I hide no secrets from you, because I love you,' say they?—eh, and their love may be anything from a mild preference to a flat lie. And so, I came finally to concede that all women are creatures of like frailties and limitations and reserves as myself, and I was most poignantly lonely when I was luckiest in love. Once only, in my life in the flesh, it seemed to me that a woman, whom I had abandoned, held in her hand the sigil visibly. That memory has often troubled me, Ettarre. It may be that this woman could have given me what I sought everywhere in vain. But I did not know this until it was too late, until the chance and the woman's life alike were wasted. . . . And so, I grew apathetic, senseless and without any spurring aspiration, seeing that all human beings are so securely locked in the prison of their flesh."

The girl replied: "When immortals visit earth it is necessary they assume the appearance of some animal. Very long ago, as we have seen, Horvendile, was discovered that secret, which so many myths veil thinly: and have we not learned, too, that the animal's fleshly body is a disguise which it is possible to put aside?"

He said: "That knowledge, so fearfully purchased at the Sabbat, still troubles me, Ettarre. Yes, it is perturbing to be assured I am only a garment which is sometimes worn by that Horvendile who is of the Léshy, and who shifts other puppets than I can imagine. For I am an overweening garment, Ettarre,—or rather, let us say, I flauntingly esteem myself a fine feather in the cap of this eternal Horvendile. So does it sometimes seem to my vainglorious self-conceit that even this demiurgic Horvendile and his Poictesme, and, for that matter, all the living anywhere in this world, are only the notions of a certain fat and flabby dreamer—"

"Nobody can think that, dear Horvendile, so long as he recalls the Sabbat—"

"Indeed," said Kennaston, in startled haste, "I am not likely to forget the Sabbat. . . . Monsieur le Prince, I regret the circumstance, but—as you see—my snuff-box is quite empty. Ah, but yes, as you very justly observe, rappee, repose and rationality are equally hard to come by in these mad days. . . . Is that not droll, Ettarre? This unvenerable old Prince de Gâtinais—once Grand Duke of Noumaria, you remember,—has in his career been guilty of every iniquity and meanness and cowardice: now, facing instant death, he finds time to think of snuff and phrase-making. . . . But—to go back a little,—I had thought the Sabbat would be so different! One imagined there would be cauldrons, and hags upon prancing broomsticks, and a black Goat, of course—"

"How much more terrible it is," the girl replied,—"and how beautiful!"

"Yet—in despite of that which the Sabbat revealed,—even now I may not touch you, Ettarre."

"My friend, all men have striven to do that; and I have evaded each one of them at the last, and innumerable are the ways of my elusion. There is no man but has loved me, no man that has forgotten me, and none but has attempted to express that which he saw and understood when I was visible."

"Do I not know?" the man said, unhappily. "There is no beauty in the world save those stray hints of you, Ettarre. Canvas and stone and verse speak brokenly of you sometimes; all music yearns toward you, Ettarre, all sunsets whisper of you, and it is because they awaken memories of you that the eyes of all children so obscurely trouble and delight us. Ettarre, your unattainable beauty tears my heart. There is nothing, nothing in me, that does not cry out for love of you. And it is the cream of a vile jest that I am forbidden ever to win quite to you, ever to touch you, ever to see you even save in my dreams!"

"Already this dream draws toward an end, my poor Horvendile."

And he saw that the great doors—which led to death,—were unclosing: and beyond them he saw confusedly a mob of red-capped men, of malignant frenzied women, of wide-eyed little children, and the staid officials, chatting pleasantly among themselves, who came to fetch that day's tale of those condemned to the guillotine. But more vividly Kennaston saw Ettarre, and saw how tenderly she smiled, in thin wintry sunlight, as she touched Kennaston upon the breast, so that the dream might end and he might escape the guillotine.

CHAPTER **34**

Of One Enigma That Threatened to Prove Allegorical

THEN again Kennaston stood alone before a tall window, made up of many lozenge-shaped panes of clear glass set in lead framework. He had put aside one of the two great curtains—of a very fine stuff like gauze, stitched over with transparent glittering beetle-wings, and embroidered with tiny seed pearls,—which hung before this window.

Snow covered the expanse of house-tops without, and the sky without was glorious with chill stars. That white city belonged to him, he knew, with a host of other cities. He was the strongest of kings. People dreaded him, he knew; and he wondered why anyone should esteem a frail weakling such as he to be formidable. The hand of this great king—his own hand, that held aside the curtain before him,—was shriveled and colorless as lamb's wool. It was like a horrible bird-claw.

("But then I have the advantage of remembering the twentieth century," he thought, fleetingly, *"and all my contemporaries are superstitious ignorant folk. It is strange, but in this dream I appear to be an old man. That never happened before.")*

A remote music resounded in his ears, and cloying perfumes were about him. . . .

"I want to be happy. And that is impossible, because there is no happiness anywhere in the world. I, a great king, say this—I, who am known in unmapped lands, and before whom nations tremble. For there are but three desirable things in life,—love and power and wisdom: and I, the king, have sounded the depths of these, and in none is happiness."

Despairing words came to him now, and welled to his lips, in a sort of chaunt:

"I am sad to-night, for I remember that I once loved a woman. She was white as the moon; her hair was a gold cloud; she had untroubled eyes. She was so fair that I longed for her until my heart was as the heart of a God. But she sickened and died: worms had their will of her, not I. So I took other women, and my bed was never lonely. Bright poisonous women were brought to me, from beyond the sunset, from the Fortunate Islands, from Invallis and Planasia even; and these showed me nameless endearments and many curious perverse pleasures. But I was not able to forget that woman who was denied me because death had taken her: and I grew a-weary of love, for I perceived that all which has known life must suffer death.

"There was no people anywhere who could withstand my armies. We traveled far in search of such a people. My armies rode into a country of great heat and endless sands, and contended with the Presbyter's brown horsemen, who fought with arrows and brightly painted bows; and we slew them. My armies entered into a land where men make their homes in the shells of huge snails, and feed upon white worms which have black heads; and we slew them. My armies passed into a land where a people that have no language dwell in dark caves under the earth, and worship a stone that has sixty colors; and we slew them, teaching ruthlessly that all which has known life must suffer death.

"Many stiff-necked kings, still clad in purple and scarlet and wearing gold crowns—monarchs whose proud faces, for all that these men were my slaves, kept their old fashion and stayed changeless as the faces of statues,—such were my lackeys: and I burned walled cities. Empires were my playthings, but I had no son to inherit after me. I had no son—only that horrible, blue, smashed and bleeding thing, born dead, that I remember seeing very long ago where the woman I loved lay dead. That would have been my son had the thing lived,—a greater and a nobler king than I. But death willed otherwise: the life that moved in me was not to be perpetuated: and so, the heart in my body grew dried and little and shriveled, like a parched pea: for I perceived that all which has known life must suffer death.

"Then I turned from warfare, and sought for wisdom. I learned all that it is permitted any man to know—oh, I learned more than is permissible. Have I not summoned demons from the depths of the sea, and at the Sabbat have I not smitten haggard Gods upon the cheek? Yea, at Phigalia did I not pass beneath the earth and strive with a terrible Black Woman, who had the head of a horse, and wrest from her what I desired to know? Have I not talked with Morskoï, that evil formless ruler of the Sea-Folk, and made a compact with him? And has not even Phobetor, whose real name may not be spoken, revealed to me his secrets, at a paid price of which I do not care to think, now I perceive that all which has known life must suffer death?

"Yea, by the Hoofs of the Goat! it seems to me that I have done these things; yet how may I be sure? For I have learned, too, that all man's senses lie to him, that nothing we see or hear or touch is truthfully reported, and that the visible world at best stands like an island in an uncharted ocean which is a highway, none the less, for much alien traffic. Yet, it seems to me that I found means whereby the universe I live in was stripped of many veils. It seems to me that I do not regret having done this. . . . But presently I shall be dead, and all my dearly-purchased, wearily-earned wisdom must lie quiet in a big stone box, and all which has known life must suffer death.

"For death is mighty, and against it naught can avail: it is terrible and strong and cruel, and a lover of bitter jests. And presently, whatever I have done or studied or dreamed, I must lie helpless where worms will have their will of me, and neither the worms nor I will think it odd, because we have both learned—by how countless attestings!—that all which has known life must suffer death."

A remote music resounded in his ears, and cloying perfumes were about him. Turning, he saw that the walls of this strange room were of iridescent lacquer, worked with bulls and apes and parrots in raised gold: black curtains screened the doors: and the bare floor was of smooth sea-green onyx.

Moreover a woman stood there who did not speak, but only waited. So did he perceive what terror was, for terror possessed him utterly; and yet he was elated, in the while that he said,—

"You have come, then, at last. . . ."

"To you at last I have come as I come to all men," she answered, "in my good hour." Then Ettarre's hands, gleaming and half-hidden with jewels, reached toward his hands, so gladly raised to hers; and the universe seemed to fold about him, just as a hand closes.

Was it as death she came to him in this dream?—as death made manifest as man's liberation from much vain toil? Kennaston, at least, preferred to think his dreams were not degenerating into such hackneyed, crude, misleading allegories. . . . Or perhaps it was as the ghost of that dead woman whom the king had loved, and must love forever, that Ettarre had come, to guide him very tenderly out of his kingdom in this world, now that the king was age-stricken and near to death, for in this one dream alone Kennaston had seemed to be an old man.

Kennaston could not ever be sure. The broken dream remained an enigma. But he got sweet terror and happiness of the dream, for all that, tasting his moment of inexplicable, poignant emotion; and therewith he was content.

CHAPTER **35**

Treats of Witches, Mixed Drinks and the Weather

MEANWHILE, I used to see Kennaston nearly every day. . . . Looking back, I recollect one afternoon when the Kennastons were calling on us. It was the usual sort of late-afternoon call customarily exchanged by country neighbors. . . .

"We have been intending to come over for ever so long," Mrs. Kennaston explained. "But we have been in such a rush, getting ready for the summer—"

"We only got the carpets up yesterday," my wife assented. "Riggs just kept promising and promising but he did finally get a man out—"

"Well, the roads are in pretty bad shape," I suggested, "and those vans are fearfully heavy—"

"Still, if they would just be honest about it," Mrs. Kennaston bewailed,—"and not keep putting you off—No, I really don't think I ever saw the Loop road in worse condition—"

"It's the long rainy spell we ought to have had in May," I informed her. "The seasons are changing so, though, nowadays that nobody can keep up with them."

"Yes, Felix was saying only to-day," Mrs. Kennaston observed, with a bright smile, "that we seem no longer to have any real spring. We simply go straight from winter into summer."

"I was endeavoring to persuade her," Kennaston emended, "that it was foolish to go away as long as it stays cool as it is."

"Oh, yes, *now!*" my wife conceded. "But the paper says we are in for a long heat period about the fifteenth. For my part, I think July is always our worst month."

"It is just that you feel the heat so much more during the first warm days," I suggested.

"Oh, no!" my wife said, earnestly; "the nights are cool in August, and you can stand the days. Of course, there are apt to be a few mosquitos in September, but not many if you are careful about standing water—"

"The drain-pipe to the gutter around our porch got stopped somehow, last year"—this Kennaston contributed, morosely,—"and we had a terrible time."

"—Then there is always so much to do, getting the children started at school," my wife continued,—"everything under the sun needed at the last moment, of course! And the way they change all the school-books every year is simply ridiculous. So, if I had my way, we would always go away early, and be back again in good time to get things in shape—"

"Oh, yes, if we could have our way!"—Mrs. Kennaston could not deny that,—"but don't your servants always want August off, to go home? I know ours do: and, my dear, you simply don't dare say a word."

"That is the great trouble in the country," I philosophized,—"in fact, we suburbanites are pretty well hag-ridden by our dusky familiars. The old-time darkies are dying out, and the younger generation is simply worthless. And with no more sense of gratitude—Why, Moira hired a new girl last week, to help out upstairs, and the very first evening—"

"No, dear, it was in the morning," my wife corrected me, "and everybody knows that the upstairs-girl everywhere used to help out with the cooking quite regularly—"

"Of course they did," Mrs. Kennaston remarked, with unconcealed indignation. "But now, even with the politest of them, you simply never know where you are. For what with the way they leave you, without one minute's notice, hag-ridden, Mr. Harrowby, is really not any name for it. They just go!"

"Oh, yes, hag-ridden! like the unfortunate magicians in old stories!" Kennaston broke in, on a sudden. "We were speaking about such things the other day, you remember? I have been thinking—You see, everyone tells me that, apart from being a master soapboiler, Mr. Harrowby, you are by way of being an authority on witchcraft and similar murky accomplishments?" And he ended with that irritating little noise, that was nearly a snigger, and just missed being a cough.

"It so often comes over me," says Moira—which happens to be my wife's name—"that Dick, all by himself, is really Harrowby & Sons, Inc."—she spoke as if I were some sort of writing fluid,—"and has his products on sale all over the world. I look on him in a new light, so to speak, when I realize that daily he is gladdening Calcutta with his soaps, delighting London with his dentifrice, and comforting Nova Zembla with his talcum powder."

"Well, but I inherited all that. It isn't fair to fling ancestral soap-vats in my face," I reminded her. "And yes, I have dabbled a bit in forces that aren't as yet thoroughly understood, Mr. Kennaston. I wouldn't go so far as to admit to witchcraft, though. Very certainly I never attended a Sabbat."

I recollect, now, how his face changed. "And what in heaven's name was a Sabbat?" Then he fidgeted, and crossed his legs the other way.

I replied: "Well! it was scarcely Heaven's name that was invoked there, if old tales are to be trusted. Traditionally, the Sabbat was a meeting attended by all witches in satisfactory diabolical standing, lightly attired in smears of various magical ointments; and their vehicle of transportation to these outings was, of course, the traditional broomstick. Good Friday night," I continued, seeing they all seemed willing enough to listen, "was the favorite time for such gatherings, which were likewise held after dusk on St. John's Eve, on Walburga's Eve, and on Hallowe'en Night. The diversions were numerous: there was feasting, with somewhat unusual fare, and music, and dancing, with the Devil performing obbligatos on the pipes or a cittern, and not infrequently preaching a burlesque sermon. He usually attended in the form of a monstrous goat; and—when not amorously inclined,—often thrashed the witches with their own broomsticks. The more practical pursuits of the evening included the opening of graves, to despoil dead bodies of finger- and toe-joints, and portions of the winding-sheet, with which to prepare a powder that had strange uses. . . . But the less said of that, the better. Here, also, the Devil taught his disciples how to make and christen statues of clay or wax, so that by roasting these effigies the persons whose names they bore would be wasted away by sickness."

"I see," said Kennaston, intently regarding his fingernails: "they must have been highly enjoyable social outings, all around."

"They must have been worse than family reunions," put in Mrs. Kennaston, and affected to shudder.

"Indeed, there are certain points of resemblance," I conceded, "in the general atmosphere of jealous hostility and the ruthless digging-up of what were better left buried."

Then Kennaston asked carelessly, "But how could such absurd superstitions ever get any hold on people, do you suppose?"

"That would require rather a lengthy explanation—Why, no," I protested, in answer to his shrug; "the Sabbat is not inexplicable. Hahn-Kraftner's book, or Herbert Perlin's either, will give you a very fair notion of what the Sabbat really was,—something not in the least grotesque, but infinitely more awe-inspiring than is hinted by any traditions in popular use. And Le Bret, whom bookdealers rightly list as 'curious'—"

"Yes, I have read those books, it happens. My uncle had them, you know. But"—Kennaston was plainly not quite at ease,—"but, after all, is it not more wholesome to dismiss such theories as fantastic nonsense, even if they are perfectly true?"

"Why, not of necessity," said I. "As touches what we call the 'occult,' delusion after delusion has been dissipated, of course, and much jubilant pother made over the advance in knowledge. But the last of his delusions, which man has yet to relinquish, is that he invented them. This too must be surrendered with time; and already we are beginning to learn that many of these wild errors are the illegitimate children of grave truths. Science now looks with new respect on folk-lore—"

"Mr. Kennaston," says Moira, laughing, "I warn you, if you start Dick on his hobbies, he will talk us all to death. So, come into the house, and I will mix you two men a drink."

And we obeyed her, and—somehow—got to talking of the recent thunderstorms, and getting in our hay, and kindred topics.

Yes, it was much the usual sort of late-afternoon call customarily exchanged by country neighbors. I remember Moira's yawning as she closed the cellarette, and her wondering how Mrs. Kennaston could keep on rouging and powdering at her age, and why Kennaston never had anything in particular to say for himself?

"Do you suppose it is because he has a swelled head over his little old book, or is he just naturally stupid?" she wanted to know.

PART SIX

**Which indicates that Lichfield
may stand not far from
Poictesme**

"Alas! the sprite that haunts us
Deceives our rash desire;
It whispers of the glorious gods,
And leaves us in the mire:

"We cannot learn the cipher
Inscribed upon our cell;
Stars taunt us with a mystery
Which we lack lore to spell."

CHAPTER 36

Sundry Disclosures of the Press

SUCH as has been described was now Felix Kennaston's manner of living, which, as touches utilitarian ends, it might be wiser forthwith to dismiss as bred by the sickly fancies of an idle man bemused with unprofitable reading. By day his half of the sigil lay hidden in the library, under a pile of unused bookplates. But nightly this bit of metal was taken with him to bed, in order that, when held so as to reflect the candlelight—for this was always necessary,—it might induce the desired dream of Ettarre; and that, so, Horvendile would be freed of Felix Kennaston for eight hours uninterruptedly.

In our social ordering Felix Kennaston stayed worthy of consideration in Lichfield, both as a celebrity of sorts and as the owner of four bank-accounts; and colloquially, as likewise has been recorded, he was by ordinary dismissed from our patronizing discussion as having long been "queer," and in all probability "a dope-fiend." In Lichfield, as elsewhere, a man's difference from his fellows cannot comfortably be conceded except by assuming the difference to be to his discredit.

Meanwhile, the Felix Kennaston who owned two motors and had money in four banks, went with his wife about their round of decorous social duties; and the same Felix Kennaston, with leisured joy in the task, had completed *The Tinctured Veil*—which, as you now know, was woven from the dream-stuff Horvendile had fetched out of that fair country, very far from Lichfield, which is bounded by Avalon and Phaeacia and Sea-coast Bohemia, and the contiguous forests of Arden and Broceliande, and on the west of course by the Hesperides.

Then, just before *The Tinctured Veil* was published, an accident happened.

Fate, as always frugal of display, used simple tools. Kennaston, midway in dressing, found he had no more mouthwash. He went into his wife's bathroom, in search of a fresh bottle. Kathleen was in town for the afternoon, at a card party; and thus it was brought about that Kennaston found, lying in the corner of her bathroom press, and hidden by a bottle of Harrowby's No. 7 Dental Delight, the missing half of the sigil of Scoteia,—the half which Ettarre had retained. There was no doubt about it. He held it in his hand.

"Now that," said Felix Kennaston, aloud, "is rather curious."

He went into the library, and lifted the little pile of unused bookplates; and presently the two pieces of metal lay united upon his wife's dressing-table, between the manicure-set and the pincushion, forming a circle not quite three inches in diameter, just such as he had seen once upon the brow of Mother Isis, and again in the Didascalion when Ptolemy of the Fat Paunch was master of Egypt.

"So, Kathleen somehow found the other half. She has had it from the first. . . . But naturally, I never spoke of Felix Kennaston; it was forbidden, and besides, the sigil's crowning grace was that it enabled me to forget his existence. And the girl's name in the printed book is Alison. And Horvendile is such an unimportant character that Kathleen, reading the tale hastily—I thought she simply skimmed it!—did not remember that name either; and so, did not associate the dream names in any way with my book, nor with me. . . . She too, then, does not know—as yet. . . . And, for all that, Kathleen, the real Kathleen, is Ettarre—'whatsoever flesh she may wear as a garment!'. . . . Or, rather, Ettarre is to Kathleen as Horvendile—but am I truly that high-hearted ageless being? Eh, I do not know, for we touch mystery everywhere. I only know it is the cream of the jest that day by day, while that lean, busy sharp-eyed stranger, whose hands and lips my own hands and lips meet daily, because this contact has become a part of the day's routine—"

But he was standing before his wife's dressing-table, and the mirror showed him a squat insignificant burgess in shirtsleeves, with grizzled untidied hair, and mild accommodating pale eyes, and an inadequate nose, with huge nostrils, and a spacious naked-looking upper-lip. That was Felix Kennaston, so far as were concerned all other people save Kathleen. He smiled; and in the act he noted that the visual result was to make Felix Kennaston appear particularly inane and sheepish. But he knew now that did not matter. Nor did it greatly matter—his thoughts ran,—that it was never permitted any man, not even in his dreams, ever to touch the hands and lips of Ettarre.

So he left there the two pieces of metal, united at last upon his wife's dressing-table, between the manicure-set and the pincushion, where on her return she might find them, and, finding, understand all that which he lacked words to tell.

CHAPTER **37**

Considerations toward Sunset

THEN Kennaston went for a meditative walk in the abating glare of that day's portentous sunset, wherein the tree-trunks westward showed like the black bars of a grate. It was in just such a twilight that Horvendile had left Storisende. . . .

And presently he came to a field which had been mowed that week. The piled hay stood in rounded heaps suggestive to Kennaston of shaggy giant heads bursting through the soil, as in the old myth of Cadmus and the dragon's teeth; beyond were glittering cornfields, whose tremulous green was shot with brown and sickly yellow now, and which displayed a host of tassels like ruined plumes. Autumn was at hand. And as Kennaston approached, a lark—as though shot vehemently from the ground,—rose singing. Straight into the air it rose, and was lost in the sun's abating brilliance; but still you could hear its singing; and then, as suddenly, the bird dropped earthward.

Kennaston snapped his fingers. "Aha, my old acquaintance!" he said, "but now I envy you no longer!"

Then he walked onward, thinking. . . .

"What did I think of?" he said, long afterward—"oh, of nothing with any real clarity. You see—I touched mystery everywhere. . . .

"But I thought of Kathleen's first kiss, and of the first time I came to her alone after we were married, and of our baby that was born dead. . . . I was happier than I had ever been in any dream. . . . I saw that the ties of our ordinary life here in the flesh have their own mystic strength and sanctity. I comprehended why in our highest sacrament we prefigure with holy awe, not things of the mind and spirit, but flesh and blood. . . . A man and his wife, barring stark severance, grow with time to be one person, you see; and it is not so much the sort of person as the indivisibility that matters, with them. . . .

"And I thought of how in evoking that poor shadow of Ettarre which figured first in *The King's Quest*, and which later came to be the gist of all my books, I had consciously written of my dear wife as I remembered her when we were young together. My vocabulary and my ink went to the making of each book's Ettarre: but with them went Kathleen's youth and purity and tenderness and serenity and loving-kindness toward all created things save the women I had flirted with,—so that Kathleen had contributed more than I. . . .

"And I saw that the good-smelling earth about my pudgy pasty body, and my familiar home—as I turned back my pudgy pasty face toward Alcluid, bathed now in the sun's gold,—were lovely kindly places. Outside were kings and wars and thunderous zealots, and groaning, rattling thunderous printing-presses, too, that were turning off a book called *The Tinctured Veil*, whereinto had been distilled and bottled up the very best that was in Felix Kennaston; but here was just 'a citadel of peace in the heart of the trouble.' And—well, I was satisfied. People do not think very much, nor at all clearly, when they are satisfied."

But he did not walk long; for it was growing chilly, as steadily dusk deepened, in this twilight so like that in which Horvendile had left Storisende forever.

CHAPTER **38**

One Way of Elusion

KATHLEEN was seated at the dressing-table, arranging her hair, when Kennaston came again into her rooms. He went forward, and without speaking, laid one hand upon each shoulder.

Now for an instant their eyes met in the mirror; and the woman's face he saw there, or seemed to see there, yearned toward him, and was unutterably loving, and compassionate, and yet was resolute in its denial. For it denied him, no matter with what wistful tenderness, or with what wonder at his folly. Just for a moment he seemed to see that; and then he doubted, for Kathleen's lips lifted complaisantly to his, and Kathleen's matter-of-fact face was just as he was used to seeing it.

And thus, with no word uttered, Felix Kennaston understood that his wife must disclaim any knowledge of the sigil of Scoteia, should he be bold enough to speak of it. He knew he would never dare to speak of it in that constricted hide-bound kindly life which he and Kathleen shared in the flesh. To speak of it would mean to become forthwith what people glibly called insane. So Horvendile and Ettarre were parted for all time. And Kathleen willed this, no matter with what wistful tenderness, and because of motives which he would never know,—for how could one tell what was going on inside that small round head his hand was caressing? Still, he could guess at her reasons;

and he comprehended now that Ettarre had spoken a very terrible truth.—"*All men I must evade at the last, and innumerable are the ways of my elusion.*"

"Well, dear," he said, aloud; "and was it a pleasant party?"

"Oh, so-so," Kathleen conceded; "but it was rather a mixed crowd. Hadn't you better hurry and change your clothes, Felix? It is almost dinner-time, and, you know, we have seats for the theater to-night."

Quite as if he, too, were thinking of trifles, Felix Kennaston took up the two bits of metal. "I have often wondered what this design meant," he said, idly,—not looking at her, and hopeful that they were at least permitted this much of allusion to what they dared not speak of openly.

"Perhaps Mr. Harrowby could tell you." Kathleen also spoke as if with entire indifference,—not looking at him, but into the mirror, and giving deft final touches to her hair.

"Eh—?" Kennaston smiled. "Oh, yes, Dick Harrowby, I grant you, has dabbled a bit in occult matters, but hardly deep enough, I fancy, to explain—this."

"At all events," Kathleen considered, "it is a quarter to seven already, and we have seats for the theater to-night."

He cleared his throat. "Shall I keep this, or you?"

"Why, for heaven's sake—! The thing is of no value now, Felix. Give it to me." She dropped the two pieces of metal into the waste-basket by the dressing-table, and rose impatiently. "Of course if you don't *mean* to change for dinner—"

He shrugged and gave it up.

So they dined alone together, sharing a taciturn meal, and duly witnessed the drolleries of *The Gutta-Percha Girl*. Kennaston's sleep afterward was sound and dreamless.

CHAPTER **39**

Past Storisende Fares the Road of Use and Wont

HE read *The Tinctured Veil* in print, with curious wistful wonder. "How did I come to write it?" was his thought. . . . And thereafter Felix Kennaston wrote no more books. He revised painstakingly, for the uniform edition of his works, the "privately printed" volumes of his remote youth; he collected a body of miscellaneous verse in the curiously unequal *Chimes at Midnight:* but after *The Tinctured Veil* he wrote nothing more save only those occasional papers which later were assembled in *How Many Angels.* "I am afraid to write against the author of *Men Who Loved Alison,*" he was wont flippantly to declare. And a few of us suspected even then that he spoke the plain truth.

For this Kennaston, to us, seemed like an instrument that had been used to accomplish a needed bit of work, and, when the work was done, had been put by. And he did not matter: what only mattered was the fact that we possessed *Men Who Loved Alison.* A quota of youngsters here and there, I know, begin to assert that we have in *The Tinctured Veil* an affair of even more grave importance, and they may be right. It is a question which will for our generation remain unsettled.

Meanwhile, Mr. and Mrs. Kennaston continued their round of decorous social duties: their dinner-parties were chronicled in the *Lichfield Courier-Herald;* and Kennaston delivered, by request, two scholarly addresses before the Lichfield Woman's Club, he was duly brought forward to shake hands with all celebrities who visited the city, and he served acceptably in the vestry of his church.

Was Felix Kennaston content?—that is a question he alone could have answered.

"But why shouldn't I have been?" he said, a little later, in reply to the pointblank query. "I had a handsome home, two motors, money in four banks, and a good-looking wife who loved and coddled me. The third prince gets no more at the end of any fairy tale. Still, the old woman spoke the truth, of course,—one pays as one goes out. . . . Oh, yes, one pays!—that is an inevitable rule; but what you have to pay is not exorbitant, all things considered. . . . So, be off with your crude pessimisms, Harrowby!"

And indeed, when one comes to think, he was in no worse case than any other husband of his standing. "Who wins his love must lose her," as no less tunefully than wisely sings one of our poets—a married bard, you may be sure,—and all experience tends to prove his warbling perfectly veracious. Romancers, from Time's nonage, have invented and have manipulated a host of staple severances for their puppet lovers,—sedulously juggling, ever since Menander's heyday, with compromising letters and un-scrupulous rivals and shipwrecks and wills and testy parents and what not,—and have contrived to show love over-riding these barriers plausibly enough. But he would truly be a boldfaced rhapsodist who dared at outset to unite his chosen pair of puppet lovers,—I mean, in plain prosaic marriage, with each other,—and then to depict their love as surviving their union, unchanged.

I am thus digressing, in obsolete Thackerayan fashion, to twaddle about love-matches alone. People marry through a variety of other reasons, and with varying results: but to marry for love is to invite inevitable tragedy. There needs no side-glancing here at such crass bankruptcies of affection as end in homicide or divorce proceedings, or even just in daily squabbling: these dramas are of the body. They may be taken as the sardonic comedies, or, at their most outrageous, as the blustering cheap melodramas, of existence; and so lie beyond the tragic field. For your true right tragedy is enacted on the stage of a man's soul, with the man's reason as lone auditor.

And being happily married—but how shall I word it? Let us step into the very darkest corner. Now, my dear Mr. Grundy, your wife is a credit to her sex, an ornament to her circle, and the mainstay of your home; and you, sir, are proverbially the most complacent and uxorious of spouses. But you are not, after all, married to the girl you met at the chancel rail, so long and long ago, with unforgotten tremblings of the knees. Your wife, that estimable matron, is quite another person. And you live in the same house, and you very often see her with hair uncombed, or even with a disheveled temper; you are familiar with her hours of bathing, her visits to the dentist, and a host of other physical phenomena we need not go into; she does not appreciate your jokes; she peeps into your personal correspondence; she keeps the top bureau-drawer in a jumble of veils and gloves and powder-rags and hair-pins and heaven knows what; her gowns continually require to be buttoned up the back* in an insane incalcuable fashion; she irrationally orders herring for breakfast, though you never touch it:— and, in fine, your catalogue of disillusionments is endless.

Hand upon heart, my dear Mr. Grundy, is this the person to whom you despatched those letters you wrote before you were married? Your wife has those epistles safely put away somewhere, you may depend on it: and for what earthly consideration would you read them aloud to her? Some day, when one or the other of you is dead, those letters will ring true again, and rouse a noble sorrow; and the survivor will be all the better for reading them. But now they only prove you were once free of uplands which you do not visit nowadays: and this common knowledge is a secret every wife must share half-guiltily with her husband—even in your happiest matrimonial ventures,—as certainly as it is the one topic they may not ever discuss with profit.

For you are married, you and she: and you live, contentedly enough, in a four-square world, where there is the rent and your social obligations and the children's underclothing to be considered, long and long before indulgence in rattle-pate mountain-climbing. And people glibly think of you as Mr. and Mrs. Grundy now, almost as a unit: but do you really know very much about that woman whose gentle breathing—for we will not crudely call it snoring,—you are privileged, now, to hear every night until the one or the other of you is done with breathing? Suppose, by a wild flight of fancy, that she is no more honest with you than you are with her?

---

* One preserves with vast pleasure this archaic quaint touch.

So to Kennaston his wife remained a not unfriendly mystery. They had been as demi-gods for a little while; and the dream had faded, to leave it matters not what memories; and they were only Mr. and Mrs. Felix Bulmer Kennaston. Of all of us, my fellow failures in the great and hopeless adventure of matrimony, this apologue is narrated.

Yet, as I look into my own wife's face—no more the loveliest, but still the dearest of all earthly faces, I protest,—and as I wonder how much she really knows about me, or the universe at large, and have not the least notion,—why, then I elect to believe that, in the ultimate, Kennaston was not dissatisfied. For each and all of us the dream-haze merges into the glare of common day; the *dea certé*, whom that fled roseate light transfigured, stands confessed a simple loving woman, a creature of like flesh and limitations as our own: but who are we to mate with goddesses? It is enough that much in us which is not ever to be measured by the strait tenets of common-sense has for once found exercise—has had its high-pitched outing, howsoever fleet,—and that, because of many abiding memories, we know, assuredly, the way of all flesh is not merely a futile scurrying through dining-rooms and offices and shops and parlors, and thronged streets and restaurants, "and so to bed."

CHAPTER **40**

Which Mr. Flaherty Does Not Quite Explain

WITH the preceding parchment I wish I might end the story. For what follows—which is my own little part in the story of Felix Kennaston,—is that discomfortable sort of anticlimax wherein the key to a mystery, by unlocking unsuspected doors, discloses only another equally perplexing riddle.

Kathleen Kennaston died in her sleep some eleven months after her husband discovered the missing half of the sigil. . . .

"I have a sort of headache," she said, toward nine o'clock in the evening. "I believe I will go to bed, Felix."

So she kissed him good-night, in just that emotionless preoccupied fashion which years of living together had made familiar; and so she left him in the music-room, to smoke and read magazines. He never saw her living any more.

Kathleen stopped in the hall, to wind the clock. "Don't forget to lock the front door when you come up, Felix." She was out of sight, but he could hear her, as well as the turning of the clock key. "I forgot to tell you I saw Adèle Van Orden to-day, at Greenberg's. They are going down to the Beach Thursday. She told me they hadn't had a cook for three days now, and she and old Mrs. Haggage have had to do all the work. She looked it, too,—I never saw any one let themselves go all to pieces the way she has—"

"How—? Oh, yes," he mumbled, intent upon his reading; "it is pretty bad. Don't many of them keep their looks as you do, dear—"

And that was all. He never heard his wife's voice any more. Kennaston read contentedly for a couple of hours, and went to bed. It was in the morning the maid found Mrs. Kennaston dead and cold. She had died in her sleep, quite peacefully, after taking two headache powders, while her husband was contentedly pursuing the thread of a magazine story through the advertising columns. . . .

Kennaston had never spoken to her concerning the sigil. Indeed, I do not well see how he could have dared to do so, in view of her attitude in a world so opulent in insane asylums. But among her effects, hidden away as before in the press in her bathroom, Kennaston found both the pieces of metal. They were joined together now, forming a perfect circle, but with the line of their former separation yet visible.

He showed me the sigil of Scoteia, having told this tale. . . .

I had thought from the first there would prove to be supernal double-dealing back of all this. The Wardens of Earth sometimes unbar strange windows, I suspect,— windows which face on other worlds than ours; and They permit this or that man to peer out fleetingly, perhaps, just for the joke's sake; since always They humorously contrive matters so this man shall never be able to convince his fellows of what he has seen, or of the fact that he was granted any peep at all. The Wardens without fail arrange what we call—gravely, too,—"some natural explanation."

Kennaston showed me the sigil of Scoteia, having told this tale. . . .

"You are interested in such things, you see,—just as Kathleen said. And I have sometimes wondered if when she said, 'Perhaps Mr. Harrowby could tell you,' the words did not mean more than they seemed then to mean—?"

I was interested now, very certainly. But I knew that Kathleen Kennaston had referred not at all to my interest in certain of the less known sides of existence, which people loosely describe as "occult."

And slowly, I comprehended that for the thousandth time the Wardens of Earth were uncompromised; that here too They stayed unconvicted of negligence in Their duty: for here was at hand the "natural explanation." Kennaston's was one of those curious, but not uncommon, cases of self-hypnosis, such as Fehlig and Alexis Bidoche have investigated and described. Kennaston's first dream of Ettarre had been an ordinary normal dream, in no way particularly remarkable; and afterward, his will to dream again of Ettarre, co-operating with his queer reading, his temperament, his idle life, his belief in the sigil, and co-operating too—as yet men may not say just how,—with the hypnotic effects of any small bright object when gazed at steadily, had been sufficient to induce more dreams. I could understand how it had all befallen in consonance with hackneyed laws, insane as was the outcome.

And the prelate and the personage had referred, of course, to the then-notorious nineteenth and twentieth chapters of *Men Who Loved Alison*, in which is described the worship of the sigil of Scoteia,—and which chapters they, in common with a great many other people, considered unnecessarily to defile a noble book. The coincidence of the mirrors was quaint, but in itself came to less than nothing; for as touches the two questions as to white pigeons, the proverb alluded to by the personage, concerning the bird that fouls its own nest, is fairly familiar, and the prelate's speech was the most natural of prosaic inquiries. What these two men had said and done, in fine, amounted to absolutely nothing until transfigured, in the crucible of an ardent imagination, by the curious literary notion that human life as people spend it is purposeful and clearly motived.

For what Kennaston showed me was the metal top of a cold cream jar. I am sure of this, for Harrowby's Crême Cleopatre is one of the most popular articles our firm manufactures. I hesitate to tell you how many thousand husbands may find at will among their wives' possessions just such a talisman as Kennaston had discovered. I myself selected the design for these covers when the stuff was first put in the market. They are sealed on, you may remember, with gray wax, to carry out the general idea that we are vending old Egyptian secrets of beauty. And the design upon these covers, as I have since been at pains to make sure, is in no known alphabet.

P. N. Flaherty (the artist implicated) tells me he "just made it up out of his head,"—blending meaningless curlicues and dots and circles with an irresponsible hand, and sketching a crack across all, "just to make it look ancient like." It was along this semblance of a fracture—for there the brittle metal is thinnest,—that the cover first picked up by Kennaston had been broken. The cover he showed me was, of course, complete. . . . So much for Mr. Flaherty's part in the matter; and of hieroglyphic lore, or any acquaintance with heathenry beyond his gleanings from the moving pictures, I would be the last person to suspect him.

It was natural that Mrs. Kennaston should have used Harrowby's Crême Cleopatre habitually; for indeed, as my wife had often pointed out, Mrs. Kennaston used a considerable amount of toilet preparations. And that Mrs. Allardyce should have had a jar of Harrowby's Crême Cleopatre in her handbag was almost inevitable: there is no better restorative and cleanser for the complexion, after the dust and dirt of a train-journey, as is unanimously acknowledged by Harrowby & Sons' advertisements.

But there is the faith that moves mountains, as we glibly acknowledge with unconcernment as to the statement's tremendous truth; and Felix Kennaston had believed in his talisman implicitly from the very first. Thus, through his faith, and through we know not what soul-hunger, so many long hours, and—here is the sardonic point,—so many contented and artistically-fruitful hours of Kennaston's life in the flesh had been devoted to contemplation of a mirage. It was no cause for astonishment that he had more than once surprised compassion and wonder in his wife's eyes: indeed, she could hardly have failed to suspect his mind was affected; but, loving him, she had tried to shield him, as is the way of women. . . .

In brief, I found the whole matter droll and rather heart-breaking. But the Wardens of Earth were uncompromised, so far as I could prove. Whatever windows had or had not been unbarred, there remained no proof. . . .

So I shook my head. "Why, no," said I, with at worst a verbal adhesion to veracity, "I, for one, do not know what the design means. Still, you have never had this deciphered," I added, gently. "Suppose—suppose there had been some mistake, Mr. Kennaston,—that there was nothing miraculous about the sigil, after all—?"

I cannot tell you of his expression; but it caused me for the moment to feel disconcertingly little and obtuse.

"Now, how can you say that, I wonder!" he marveled,—and then, of course, he fidgeted, and crossed his legs the other way,—"when I have been telling you, from alpha to omega, what is the one great thing the sigil taught me—that everything in life is miraculous. For the sigil taught me that it rests within the power of each of us to awaken at will from a dragging nightmare of life made up of unimportant tasks and tedious useless little habits, to see life as it really is, and to rejoice in its exquisite wonderfulness. If the sigil were proved to be the top of a tomato-can, it would not alter that big fact, nor my fixed faith. No, Harrowby, the common names we call things by do not matter,—except to show how very dull we are," he ended, with that irritating noise that was nearly a snigger, and just missed being a cough.

Then he was silent. Evening was approaching now, and twilight gathered in the room. But as Kennaston sat there looking down into the open fire, its glow made plainly visible his pudgy and vacuous face. . . .

And I was sorely tempted. . . . You see, I never liked Felix Kennaston. The man could create beauty, to outlive him; but in his own appearance he combined grossness with insignificance, and he added thereto a variety of ugly senseless little mannerisms. He could evolve interesting ideas, as to Omnipotence, the universe, art, life, religion, himself, his wife, a candlestick or a comet—anything,—and very probably as to me; but his preferences and his limitations would conform and color all these ideas until they were precisely what he desired to believe, no more or less; and, having them, he lacked means, or courage, to voice his ideas adequately, so that to talk with him meant a dull interchange of commonplaces. Again, he could aspire toward chivalric love, that passion which sees in woman-kind High God made manifest in the loveliest and most perfect of His creations; but in the quest he had succeeded merely in utilizing womenfolk either as toys to play with and put by or as drudges to wait on him; yet, with all this, he could retain unshaken his faith in and his worship of that ideal woman. He could face no decision without dodging; no temptation without compromise; and he lied, as if by instinct, at the threatened approach of discomfort or of his fellows' disapproval: yet devils, men and seraphim would conspire in vain in any effort to dissuade him from his self-elected purpose. For, though he would do no useful labor he could possibly avoid, he could grudge nothing to the perfection of his chosen art, in striving to perpetuate the best as he saw it.

In short, to me this man seemed an inadequate kickworthy creature, who had muddled away the only life he was quite certain of enjoying, in contemplation of a dream; and who had, moreover, despoiled the lives of others, too, for the dream's sake. To him the dream alone could matter,—his proud assurance that life was not a blind and aimless business, not all a hopeless waste and confusion;

and that he, this gross weak animal, could be strong and excellent and wise, and his existence a pageant of beauty and nobility. To prove this dream was based on a delusion would be no doubt an enjoyable retaliation, for Kennaston's being so unengaging to the eye and so stupid to talk to; but it would make the dream no whit less lovely or less dear to him,—or to the rest of us, either.

For it occurred to me, as we sat together there in the firelight, with the dusk rising everywhere about us, that his history was, in essentials, the history of our race, thus far. All which I advanced for or against him, equally, was true of all men that have ever lived. . . . For it is in this inadequate flesh that each of us must serve his dream; and so, must fail in the dream's service, and must parody that which he holds dearest. To this we seem condemned, being what we are. Thus, one and all, we play false to the dream, and it evades us, and we dwindle into responsible citizens. And yet always thereafter—because of many abiding memories,—we know, assuredly, that the way of all flesh is not, not merely, a futile scurrying through dining-rooms and offices and shops and parlors, and thronged streets and restaurants, "and so to bed.". . .

It was in appropriate silence, therefore, that I regarded Felix Kennaston, as a parable. This man was not only very human: he was humanity.

THE EPILOGUE

Which is the proper ending
of all comedies; and heralds,
it may be, an afterpiece.

"The Past is over and fled;
Named new, we name it the old;
Thereof some tale hath been told,
But no word comes from the dead.

"Still we say as we go,—
'Strange to think by the way,
Whatever there is to know,
That shall we know one day.'"

The Epilogue

AND yet, sir," I had said, by and by, "yet it is only by preserving faith in human dreams that we may, after all, perhaps some day make them come true."

And Kennaston, without bothering to look toward me, had gravely inclined his head.

"In fact," he remarked, "that sums up everything nicely enough. So here upon, this note of temperate optimism —howsoever cautiously conditioned and behedged and qualified,—here let us end the long journeying of the life of Manuel. For logic now demands that of me, here and in no other place."

I was, you may depend upon it, startled. . . . I saw then that the old fellow was still looking, not at me, but into the fireplace where the red glowing seemed to detain his gaze. And I felt that this was not quite Felix Kennaston, but, rather, through the virtue of that small steady glowing, in some part Horvendile who was now talking.

"Meanwhile," he said, "that life has journeyed a far way, from the body of the Redeemer of Poictesme to the body of Felix Kennaston, and from the high turrets of Storisende to the penned-in, quiet library of Alcluid. There has been adventuring in the journey, much of it pleasant enough: the codes of chivalrous and gallant persons, and of little poets also, have been fairly tested in many lands and times: yet the comedy has not, after all, very greatly differed in any place or era."

He moved, uneasily. He sighed. He said, still looking down into the fire:

"I deduce that the thing said to Florian de Puysange by the red-headed guide of all, holds true. The comedy of the life of Manuel does not vary. The first act is the imagining of the place where contentment exists and may be come to; and the second act reveals the striving toward, and the third act the falling short of, that shining goal,—or, else, the attaining of it, to discover that happiness, after all, abides a

183

thought farther down the bogged, rocky, clogged, befogged, heart-breaking road."

To this more or less incomprehensible sort of talking I replied with quiet stubbornness. I said:

"But, even so,—and even then,—the wise will yet reflect that it is only by preserving faith in human dreams that we may, after all, perhaps some day make them come true,—and that we may thus add to the comedy of the life of man an afterpiece."

"You may be right," a strangely tired and shrunk looking Kennaston answered me, "and certainly I cannot go so far as to say that you are wrong. But, still, at the same time—! Yes, that is how I feel about it, even now. . . . In any case, the journeying must by every rule of logic end here. For the life of Manuel, housed, after twenty-two removes, in the fat body of Felix Kennaston, has, after all, regained the road to Storisende—"

At that I remarked: "I, in my turn, deduce, sir, that, now you possess—as you call the thing,—the complete sigil, you must have used it yet again, in some manner which you have never told me about?"

He said: "I have not ever employed the complete sigil. And it is true I have not told you everything. Why should I? No Author ever does. . . . So, as yet, this Kennaston waits, in the quiet library at Alcluid, mildly bored and a bit puzzled by the Lichfield in whose affairs he has somehow become involved. But an assured way out of all these drab annoyances is known to him, and the way back is known, also, to that Poictesme from which the life of Manuel a great long while ago set forth. With Felix Kennaston—or, if you prefer it so, with Horvendile,—rests safe this secret and peculiar knowledge as to how the life of Manuel may yet repair to its first home after some seven centuries of exile. Thus will the traveller return—by and by—to the place of his starting; the legend of the second coming of the Redeemer will be justified, in, at all events, my lesser world; and the tale of Manuel's life will have come again, as it did once beside the pool of Haranton, full circle."

"Alas, my friend," I observed, "if you spoke Greek or Coptic now it might be I would understand you rather better."

But I was at large pains to talk unemphatically, and to keep my voice well lowered. For it was plain enough that this pudgy, old, neurotic wreckage of a man, once more, was partly hypnotized, by gazing thus steadily into the small bright fire; and I was finding his queer borderland condition to be of some interest.

He said then: "Felix Kennaston, alone of all the Manuelides, has returned to Storisende. He too has acquired that sigil and that secret—forever unknown to you, my poor Harrowby,—through which this elderly and this rather famous person has glimpsed, howsoever brokenly, the loves and the desires and the adventures he had when he wore another body than the gray body which he now wears. And to this Felix Kennaston also has been shown—a bit tantalizingly—the face of an unforgotten boy who has been free, through seven whole centuries, to follow after his own thinking and his own desires. . . . For the comedy of the life of Manuel, I repeat, does not ever vary."

"Yet by and by," I prompted him, "you, Horvendile, will employ the complete sigil?"

"Yes, by and by," the droning, very tired voice went on. "And then a lean and snub-nosed stranger will come to me also. 'And what is that thing?' this stranger will perforce be asking, as he asks of everyone at long last. Nor can the answer ever vary, whether it be you or I or any other man who speaks at the end of his living here. 'It is the figure of a man which I have modeled and remodeled, and cannot get exactly to my liking.' . . . For thus it has been in the old days and in every day. And this is the end of every comedy. Yet—I agree with you, my Harrowby,—yet, if the Author will it, there may be appended to any comedy an afterpiece. Meanwhile, so far as I may judge, the life of Manuel ends here."

Thereafter he sat gazing rather moodily into the fire. And I too summed up in brief my entire knowledge as to this matter by saying nothing whatever.

EXPLICIT

Appendix

Variants Among First Edition (1917), Kalki Edition (1922)
(Modern Library), and Storisende Edition (1930)

This appendix charts the changes Cabell made from the first edition to the second (Kalki) to the final (Storisende). Double slash indicates end of the affected passage. If there are only two changes involved, the Kalki is the same as the First. I have tried to note all punctuation changes except the addition of the comma before the dash, which—unless noted—the reader may assume was added only for the Storisende edition. If there is an addition rather than an alteration, the page and line number indicate where in the first edition, the addition occurs. For the Kalki edition, I have used the Modern Library since that is most easily available. Pagination here for Storisende edition is to the McBride plates.

Title page in First Edition: A Comedy of Evasions // In Storisende: A Comedy of Evasion

Major divisions of First Edition are called Books, Book First, Book Second, etc. The Books are not titled. Divisions of Storisende Edition are called Parts, Part One, Part Two, etc. and are titled. Chapters are numbered within each Book of the First Edition, but consecutively throughout the Storisende without regard to division. Title page of Kalki (Modern Library) does not bear any subtitle, is still divided into Books (rather than Parts), but runs consecutively without regard to division.

Preface of the First Edition is retitled as Chapter I of the Kalki and of the Storisende, "Palliation of the Gambit." Chapter Five of Book Four (a long chapter for the book) is made into two short chapters in the Kalki and in the Storisende, the new chapter being XXVIII, "The Shallowest Sort of Mysticism."

xiii.16 change // 3.16 changing
xv.3 For I commence // 4.21 So I commence
xv.4 Count Emmerick reigned in Poictesme, having not yet blundered into the disfavor of his papal cousin Adrian VII. . . . With such // 4.22 Count Emmerick, gray Manuel's not over-glorious

son, was again ruling Poictesme, now that the rebellion of Maugis d'Aigremont appeared virtually at an end. . . . For with

xv.12 (by-and-by) // 5.1 (by and by)

4.18 however // 7.12 howsoever

5.9 She wondered at him, // 7.27 She wondered at such foolish speaking,

5.17 "My friend, // 8.5 To that, Ettarre replied: "My friend,

6.17 whom // 8.28 whom, when all is done,

6.17 eternal happiness, with smiling incredulity, as we turn back to a workaday world. // 8.29 eternal happiness, in the while that we, with smiling incredulity, get back to our workaday world.

7.13 road—and how these women's clothes are adjusted, and what they eat for breakfast, and what men have kissed them: // 9.18 road,—and I know, too, what is the good faith and the loving tenderness and the never-sleeping jealousy of these women, and how these women's clothes

8.1 has never // 10.1 has not ever

8.14 "And am I not, then, a human being?" says she. // 10.15 ¶"And am I not, then, a human being?" says she. . . .

8.23 // K:11.1 "But I had thought poets were famous for their inconstancy. It is remarkable hearing that, to the contrary, they have all loved steadfastly the same woman; and, in any case, I question how, without suspecting it, I could have been that woman." // 10.24 ¶"But," said Ettarre, "but I had

9.15 Antigonê, // 11.16 Antigone,

9.20 // 11.21 ¶ Ettarre replied,

10.23 // 12.19 ¶ Then she left him.

11.9 guards the loftiest part of the province. // K:13.8 guards the loftiest part of all Poictesme. // 13.8 guarded the loftiest part of all inhabited Poictesme.

12.10 sun, and, growing drunk // 14.6 sun, when I behold the skylark, growing drunk

13.5 // 14.23 Your shining is a ruining fire.

15.22 scribblers. // 16.16 scribblers," Maugis answered.

16.8 certainly. // 17.5 certainly . . . . And

16.10 with no recreation save to watch the turrets of Storisende on clear afternoons. // K:17.9 with no recreation except upon clear forenoons to look at the towers of Storisende." // 17.7

16.13 "Where Ettarre prepares to marry Sir Guiron," Horvendile prompted. // K:17.12 "Meanwhile at Storisende Ettarre prepares to marry Sir Guiron." // 17.10 "Meanwhile, at Storisende," said Horvendile, "Ettarre prepares to marry Sir Guiron."

16.20 that // 17.16 in order that

16.24 that, Horvendile." // K:17.22 that." // 17.20

17.1 // 17.21 Horvendile said then,

17.4 Perion, and with // K:17.25 Perion, and Heitman Michael, and with // 17.24

17.6 Then // 17.26 Now

18.15 // 18.28 ¶The barons of Poictesme had well-nigh lost the knack of dancing, during the twelve years of never-ending warfare which had been stirred up by the lust and greed of Maugis d'Aigremont: but to-night all trouble seemed to have departed from Storisende; and these warriors merrily returned to the sports of their youth.

20.12 loved!" // 21.6 trusted!"

21.8 without; // 21.24 without:

21.10 of a harborage //K:22.3 of company // 21.26

21.13 // 21.29 Horvendile replied:

21.13 heaven // K:22.5 Heaven // 21.29

21.17 certain as yet // 22.4 certain, as yet,

23.5 // 23.5 The girl said:

24.16 many wounds, Horvendile. // 24.11 many wounds.

24.17 Guiron and Perion and Emmerick // 24.11 Guiron and Michael and Perion

24.21 here. For I desire // K:24.19 too soon. I // 24.15

25.4 pensive. // K:24.26 pensive, as he said: // 24.22 pensive, as he replied:

25.9 she who was by ordinary // 24.28 she who by ordinary was

26.2 // 26.2 Sir Guiron cried to her, in the while that the maid answered:

26.5 he answered joyously. // 26.5 the tall warrior said joyously.

26.13 stayed motionless while she told Guiron of Horvendile's baleful work. // 26.11 remained wholly motionless while Ettarre spoke. She told Guiron of this Horvendile's baleful work.

26.18 Horvendile answered quietly. // 26.17 Horvendile answered, without moving, even now.

27.4 and he had loved Horvendile. // 27.1 and he had hitherto esteemed Horvendile as a competent and a quite useful servant.

27.8 shook his head, smiling. // 27.5 shook his red curls, smilingly.

27.14 purported to be translated from an old manuscript // K:27.11 he pretended to translate from an old manuscript // 27.11

27.18 writer // 27.15 maker

28.2 draws to a close." // 27.22 draws near to its ending."

28.6 course. // 27.27 course," the clerk assented.

28.16 this bright fantastic tiny land // K:28.7 this bright fantastic Poictesme // 28.7

29.17 my romance here untroubled // K:29.6 here weave out my romance untroubled // 29.4

29.20 You are all that I once meant to be, Guiron, all that I have forgotten how to be; and for a dead boy's sake I love you." // 29.6

You are all that I once meant to be, Guiron, you are all that I have
forgotten how to be; and for a dead boy's sake I have loved you
even when I shrugged at your so many chivalrous virtues."
30.3 Yet I have loved you, Horvendile, and I know that heaven,
through heaven's // K:29.15 Yet I have loved you, Horvendile, and
I know that Heaven, through Heaven's // 29.14 Yet I have thriven
by your aid; and I know that Heaven, through Heaven's
30.17 Long and long // 29.28 ¶ Long and very long
31.5 I must return into my own country and abide there always...." // 30.11 I must return into my own country."
32.13 hands, spread // 31.11 hands, he spread
32.19 // 31.18 ¶ "You will not always
33.6 he paused, looking back at Guiron and Ettarre for a
heart-beat. // 31.28 he did not pause, but he glanced back at Guiron
and Ettarre for the while of a heart-beat.
33.7 Guiron and Ettarre had already forgotten his existence.
Hand-in-hand they stood in the bright room, young, beautiful and
glad. Silently their lips met. // K:32.7 Hand in hand //32.1 ¶Guiron
and Ettarre had forgotten his existence. Hand in hand they stood
in the bright room, young, beautiful and glad. Silently their lips
met. The two had put away all sorrow. They did not know of the
gray Norns' decreeing as to Ettarre, nor of that long imprisonment
which awaited her in the Waste Beyond the Moon, nor of that
ruining which was to come of her loveliness in yet other centuries
thereafter.
33.11 left Storisende forever. // 32.10 left Storisende.
33.12 Without he came // 32.11 Without, he came
33.16 carrying half the sigil of Scoteia . . . . // 32.14 carrying away
from Storisende one half of the sigil of Scoteia . . . .
37.5 folk should call him Felix, // 35.5 he should be called Felix,
37.16 however // 35.9 howsoever
38.12 all great geniuses // 36.7 we great geniuses
38.19 roaming in twilight clasping this bauble, // K:36.16 astray in
the twilight with this picked up piece of trash, // 36.14 . . . picked-
up . . .
38.21 carrying much such a bauble. // K:36.18 carrying much such
a jigumicrank. // 36.16
41.16 which years ago // K:39.13 which had, years earlier, // 39.7
which, not long before this time,
41.17 // 39.9 [The chapter division is deleted.]
42.8 novel, even though its byways can boast of little traffic
nowdays. He // K:40.1 novel. Kennaston // 39.21
42.9 He was completing, // 39.22 Kenaston was completing,
42.14 pretense therein // K:40.6 cliché of pretending // 39.26

42.15 translated // K:40.7 "retold" // 39.27 "retold"

43.12 as extinct as velocipedes // 40.18 as uncommon as bicycles

43.20 than the life // 40.25 than did the life

43.22 For as Horvendile he lived among such gallant circumstances as he had always vaguely hoped his real life might provide to-morrow. // K:41.11 provide by and by // 40.27 This was not the first time that Kennaston had written of Ettarre and Horvendile: for *The King's Quest,* of course, tells all about the ruining which this evasive pair contrived for King Alfgar, in somewhat stodgy Spenserian verse. But Kennaston now understood this Horvendile more completely. . . . And so, as Horvendile, he now lived among such gallant circumstances as he had always vaguely hoped his real life might provide by and by.

43.24 // 41.7 ¶This Horvendile,

44.5 called of course in the printed book—seems to us in reading the tale // K:41.15 called of course in the book,—this Horvendile now seems to us no // 41.11 called, of course, in the printed book,—this Horvendile now seems to us no

44.10 writing // 41.15 while writing

44.9 But Felix Kennaston, writing the book, lived the life of Horvendile in the long happy hours of writing, which became longer and longer; and insensibly his existence blended and was absorbed into the more colorful life of Horvendile. It was as Horvendile he wrote, // K:41.22 writing, in stints which steadily became longer and more pleasurable; // 41.15 But Felix Kennaston, while writing this book, lived the strange life of Horvendile in Kennaston's long, happy hours of writing, in stints which steadily became longer and more pleasurable; and insensibly his existence blended, and was absorbed, into the more colorful life of Horvendile. It was as Horvendile that Kennaston wrote,

44.24 where Horvendile keeps his proper place as a more-or-less convenient devise for getting the tale told. // 42.1 wherefrom Ettarre has wholly disappeared, and wherein Horvendile keeps his proper place as a more or less convenient devise for getting the tale told.

45.17 as all other normal forms of life, // K:42.23 with other normal forms of life, // 42.18

47.10 obligations // K:44.9 obligements // 43.28

48.10 *tête-à-têtes* // K:45.4 tête-à-têtes // 44.21

48.20 and so, it may well be that his story // 45.1 and so it may well be that hereinafter his story

49.12 weathered before // 46.11 weathered through before

54.5 who knew // 50.5 who had known

55.23 nightmares I quite // 51.16 nightmares that I quite

56.17 // 52.9 Ettarre replied pensively:

56.17 "I never heard it before. // 52.9 "I never heard that name before.

56.22 dreams. When // 52.15 dreams. . . . When

57.4 waited patiently and alertly // 52.21 watied, patiently and alertly,

58.5 forests—how inconsequently they fret upon men's heart-strings!" // K:54.23 forests. . . . . These are the little magics, that have no large power, but how inconsequently do they fret upon men's heart-strings!" // 53.16

58.11 it is how quickly // 53.22 it is," the girl marveled, "how quickly

59.14 and, as the clock showed, it was bedtime. // 54.18 and the clock showed bedtime.

59.19 reflected; "to think // 54.21 reflected. "To think

63.13 The Gayvery // 57.27 the Gayvery

64.9 *The Apostates*, a scathing arraignment of plutocratic iniquities, which was heralded // K:59.25 *The Apostates*,—by Kennaston's own loathed first-cousin,—which guaranteed // 57.24

69.3 Then one propitious morning // 61.13 Then, one propitious morning,

69. 20 neither remember or // 61.28 neither remember nor

70.2 // 62.5 ¶Thereafter

70.23 delightful romances: // 62.24 delightful saccharine romances:

71.1 but, like all the others, // 62.26 but, like all the other Tarkingtonian tales of the triumph of honest worth in somewhat melodramatic circumstances,

71.12 *chefs d'oeuvre* // K:65.24 chefs d'oeuvre // 63.10

72.10 concerning Felix Kennaston's personality, // K:67.10 as to this Felix Kennaston's personality, // 64.9

73.5 // 64.21 And it was droll to be having so many scented letters from strange women whose designs as to his physical chastity were wholly frank.

73.19 but certainly she would never admit to either fact. // 65.13 but he well knew she would never admit either fact.

73.20 He doubted very much // 65.15 He much doubted

74.10 grapefruit; and the former poet // 65.28 grapefruit. ¶Then the former poet

74.14 when they // 66.1 when he and she

75.4 There is always something more important that has // 66.15 There is always something that simply has

75.19 // 67.1 ¶He spoke

75.22 // 67.4 ¶Isn't this

76.6 more important things // 67.10 more important and more practical topics

76.13 Then wearily, // 67.16 Then Kathleen said, with aloof weariness,

77.7 // 68.6 So he answered:

77.7 // 68.7 ¶"When you insisted

77.12 remarks— // 68.12 remarks,

77.22 // 68.22 ¶Pleased with

77.24 // 68.23 And Kathleen said,

78.4 truth. // 68.27 truth," Kennaston admitted.

78.7 any one // 69.1 anyone

79.6 // 69.23 She returned then to the gasoline engine which was not working, she touched upon the possibility of there again being a dead frog in the well, she mentioned a number of her relatives who had herring for breakfast almost every morning, and she became emphatic as to the quite dreadful batch of persons who had been elected directors of the Woman's Club. And, as each topic arose, Felix Kennaston made one or another elaborately chilly reply, as he sat waiting, with elaborate patience, for his eggs.

79.11 reflected, "I shall // 70.7 reflected, in the while that Kathleen spoke of the sort of people that were getting into the Woman's Club nowadays,

81.4 that kingdoms did not // K:75.2 that kingdoms nowhere might // 71.22

84.8 however // 74.14 howsoever

84.10 secretary // 74.16 Secretary of State

84.12 than usual: // 74.18 than usual, now that he pointed out:

87.9 // 76.27 LINE SPACE IN TEXT BEFORE So the talk flowed on,

88.7 And not one of these much-talked about men, whatever // K:81.2 And not one of them, however distinguished, or whatever // 77.18 . . . or whatsoever

88.17 casually—beginning "That // K:81.12 casually,—through a "That // 77.28

88.21 he was able, later on, // K:81.15 he was to begin, later, // 78.2

89.8 // K:81.26 But all the while Kennaston was, really, thinking that here before him, half-revealed, shone the world-famous teeth protrayed by cartoonists in the morning-paper every day, everywhere. Yes, they were remarkable teeth—immaculate, marmoreal and massive,—and they were so close-set that Kennaston was now smitten with an idiotic desire to ask their owner if the personage could get dental floss between them. . . . // 78.14

89.16 But Kennaston's thoughts were vaguely dental. And there is no denying Kennaston was astounded. // K:82.15 Kennaston's thoughts remained, as yet, dental. But there is no denying Kennaston was perturbed. // 79.1

90.11 and a bright gleam of teeth, // K:83.5 and with more teeth than ever, // 79.18

91.21 Eugène // K:84.12 Eugene // 80.22

92.6 What could a little mirror, much less pigeons, have to do with this bit of metal?—except that this bit of metal, too, reflected light so that the strain tired eyes, thus steadily to look down upon the thing . . . . // 80.29 What could a little mirror, or, of all things, pigeons, have to do with this bit of metal?—except that this bit of metal, too, reflected light so that the strain tired your eyes, thus steadily to look down upon this time-worn glittering object. . . .

93.4 copybook; // 82.3 copybook:

93.13 // 82.14 ¶But there was

93.15 not one glimmer overhead. // K:85.14 not one glimmer. // 82.15 not one glimmer. And he was replying:

94.1 of wellnigh ducal disposition; and by preference, // K:86.1 a lover of all bodily comforts: so, by preference, // 82.19

94.19 // 83.14 He noticed that he was saying now:

94.24 is no pleasant dream o'nights. // K:86.23 blend in no pleasant dreams. . . . // 83.20

95.11 *meum* with *tuum*." // K:87.6 *tuum* with *meum*." // 84.2

96.8 // 84.22 The girl continued:

97.5 "And yet, I resist // 85.13 "And yet," the man echoed, "yet

97.12 knight, I would // 85.20 knight I would

97.17 however // 85.25 howsoever

99.6 visible now to him, // K:90.10 visible now, and she // 87.1

99.10 her hand went out gladly toward him. // K:90.14 her hand went out toward him gladly. // 87.5

103.15 Kennaston asked her. // 91.13 he asked.

105.2 Why worry over one particular inexplicable detail, // K:96.25 What need is there to worry over any one inexplicable detail, // 92.18

106.2 and, most vividly of all, that the exultance which possessed him // 93.12 and that the exultance which now possessed him

106.10 and there is not an office-building or an electric-light advertisement of chewing-gum in sight. // K:98.2 and nowhere in sight is an office-building or an electric-light advertisement of chewing-gum. // 93.19

106.17 where we may chance to be, Ettarre. // 93.24 and it will never matter, Ettarre, where we may chance to be.

108.14 Its tiny flame, // K:100.10 The tiny flame, // 95.6

109.1 He was glad now he was well-to-do, if only because, as an incidental result of materially bettered fortunes, // 95.16 He was glad now to be well-to-do, if only because, as one result of their materially bettered fortunes,

110.1 THE diurnal part // 96.1 THE day-lit part

110.14 lest it should cause you, // K:101.13 lest this workaday mask, of unamiable flesh and mannerisms, should cause you, // 96.14

112.10 But the prelate // 97.4 ¶The prelate

114.11 He paused. // 99.13 Kennaston paused.

114.11 // 99.14 ¶The prelate nodded.

114.14 coincidences, a famous // 99.17 coincidences," said Kennaston, as unconcernedly as he could manage, "a famous

115.8 He // 100.6 Now Kennaston

115.19 he said, // 100.18 the prelate continued,

116.17 "I will not tempt you, therefore, to tell me the whole truth concerning that bit of metal. I suspect, quite candidly, you are keeping something back, my son. But you exercise a privilege common to all of us." // 101.9 "I shall not tempt you, therefore, to tell me the whole truth concerning that bit of metal." ¶Oh, as to that, sir—!" ¶"You said just now," the older man continued, equably, " 'that bit of metal was to me then just a bit of metal.' There can be much virtue in a 'then.' So I suspect quite candidly, you are keeping something back. But, in doing so, you exercise a privilege common to both of us."

117.5 Kennaston // 101.26 Felix Kennaston

118.8 or lean strangers carefully and gruesomely explained the importance of the task set him by quoting fragments of the multiplication tables, or a mad bull who happened to be the King of Spain was pursuing him through a city of blind people. // K:108.7 or when thin men in black hoods carefully explained the importance of the task set him by quoting fragments of the multiplication tables, or when a bull who happened to be the King of Spain was pursuing him through a city of blind people. // 102.7

123.24 ever alter, to his knowledge, // 106.24 ever change, save only once,

128.9 those queer round boxes whence vegetation sprouted as from the soil of a planet? // K:117.2 in those queer round boxes out of which an uncanny vegetation, that people, here again, so glibly and unwonderingly called hair, was sprouting as if from the soil of a planet? // 109.22

128.21 what happened in one human head was signaled to another, // 110.5 was signaled to the lonely inhabitant of yet another one of those round boxes,

130.11 of his coronation: // 111.11 following his coronation:

130.17 // 111.17 All in all, the Emperor had got no pleasure out of his day's work.

130.17 // 111.19 ¶In a neglected orchard,

130.19 Shakespeare; // 111.21 Shakespeare:

131.3 worrying over Lord Pembroke's neglect of him, and trying to concoct a masque in the style of fat Ben Jonson, since that was evidently what the theater-patronizing public wanted. // 112.1 he was worrying over Lord Pembroke's neglect of him, and he was trying to concoct a masque in the style of fat Ben Jonson, since that was evidently what the theather-patronizing public wanted; and, working thus against the grain, Shakespeare had got not any pleasure out of his day's work.

131.7 And // 112.7 ¶Then

131.12 and chuckling with fond pride // 112.12 and he was chuckling with fond pride

131.13 questions. // 112.13 questions, because Pontius Pilate was exceedingly well pleased with his day's work.

132.15 sorcerers and // 113.11 sorcerers, and

133.6 and of // 113.25 and he read, too, of

134.15 than he ever did as to his later compositions. // 114.27 than he ever did as to some of his later compositions.

134.19 and *His Mistress* // 115.2 and to *His Mistress*

135.3 you will find // K:122.13 you can find // 115.10

136.10 whatever // 116.10 whatsoever

137.8 conscious, one by one, of a restricted number of these fractions of a second. // 117.1 conscious of a restricted number of these fractions of a second, one by one.

137.12 but meant // 117.5 but meant, instead,

137.13 by as many as possible // 117.6 by many, by as many as was possible,

137.15 complete success // 117.7 complete success in life

137.19 If only in dreams he // K:124.16 If only in dreams! he // 117.13

139.6 played with, // 118.17 when played with,

143.6 Once // 121.5 For once

143.7 and the // 121.6 then the

144.3 // 121.20 ¶Charicles,

144.5 persecutions these // 121.22 persecutions which these

144.7 disapproval. // 122.1 disapproval, and said forthwith:

146.1 Heliogabalus // K:131.16 Ela-Gabal // 123.12

147.11 three or four slender metal rods, // 124.16 a cluster of slender metal rods,

148.5 Hero // K:133.11 Heron // 125.5

148.15 portals. // 125.13 portals, so that they would unclose without human agency and would thus open her shrine to all the faithful who had attested the soundness of their faith by honoring her with burnt sacrifices.

150.4 the sole repository at this period of many // 126.4 which at this period was the sole repository of many

150.8 // 126.8 Amrou then said, as became a devout Mussulman:

150.14 done. // 126.15 done. . . .
150.19 Whatever might happen upon earth, during the existence of that midge among the planets, affected infinitesimally, if at all, the universe of which // 126.20 Whatever might happen upon earth, affected infinitesimally, if it affected at all, the revealed universe of which this planet
151.19 With the // 127.16 ¶No: with the
154.16 and at Prior Park Kennaston watched Mrs. Elizabeth Barnes, then acting as cook for Dr. William Warburton, destroy in making piecrust the unique manuscript copies of three of Shakespeare's dramas, which had never been printed. // K:138.27 [Same as in Storisende except for 1.8 p. 138 read "those very three." ed.] // 129.21 in the tidiest of old English kitchens Kennaston watched thrifty Betty Baker, then acting as cook for Warburton the anitquary, destroy in making pie-crust the unique manuscript copies of some fifty plays, among which were never-printed tragedies by Marlowe and Cyril Tourneur and George Chapman, and comedies by Middleton and Greene and Dekker, and—rather drolly,—those same three dramas which Shakespeare, when he talked with Horvendile in the orchard, had asserted to perpetuate, upon the whole, the most excellent fruit of Shakespeare's ripened craftsmanship.
154.22 And— // K:139.12 Yet— // 130.4
157.22 // 132.16 ¶Kennaston could see,
157.24 // 132.18 Meanwhile the old lean friar continued:
157.24 "For I am // 132.19 ¶"—For I am
158.6 For this period of time, // K:141.27 For one thousand years, // 132.24
158.15 perfect age of man, // 133.3 mature age of man,
159.21 Then // 134.1 THEN
160.21 everywhere, and the broth was cold. . . . // 134.24 everywhere; the King was misled by wicked advisers; and the broth was cold as a king's heart.
160.23 Thus the broken adventurer, Christoforo Colombo, mumbled. // K:144.8 Thus mumbled the broken adventurer, Cristoforo Colombo. // 134.27
161.6 And // 135.5 AND
162.2 Then, too, // 135.23 Then too,
162.11 sexes," Mistress // 136.3 sexes," therefore Mistress
162.14 whether such might happen to be legitimate or not. // 136.6 whether (as might best please Heaven's high wisdom) the King's well-beloved and most virtuous cousin should happen to bear legitimate children or bastards. True love provides against all, the King remarked.
162.15 A pension // 136.11 Moreover, a pension

162.20 the key to a certan bed-chamber, // 136.15 the key to Nan's bed-chamber,

163.15 *clichés* // K:146.14 clichés // 137.14

163.19 here, too, // 137.17 here too,

164.6 seek at once // 137.23 seek, at once,

165.4 presently // K:147.25 by and by // 138.20

165.4 silent naked // 138.21 silent, naked,

167.2 thus whimsically voicing the inquiry as to whether human beings // K:149.14 thus whimsically voicing a real desire to know if human beings // 140.5

167.22 not perhaps // 140.24 not, perhaps,

168.1 the answer to his query was written explicitly, in various books, // K:150.9 the answer to his query was, in various books, explicitly written, // 140.27

168.6 heaven. // 141.2 Heaven

168.19 source // 141.15 sources

169.12 was privileged // 142.3 was, perhaps uniquely, privileged

169.21 or in other ways // 142.12 nor did they in many other ways

169.23 and the stage; // 142.13 and of the stage;

170.7 Meanwhile they had // 142.22 ¶They had meanwhile

170.24 existence—to-morrow. // 143.8 existence to-morrow.

171.7 as their priests // 143.16 and this was the sole point upon which their priests

171.10 —would be quite different. // 143.19 —to-morrow would be quite different.

171.15 and it was this, precisely, that you were to disregard. // 143.25 and it was in the insignificance of this moment, precisely, that pious people must believe.

171.16 Such was the burden // K:153.13 So ran the teachings // 143.26

173.13 // 146.8 ¶Later,

174.1 however unready posterity stood // K:155.23 however unapt might be posterity // 146.19 howsoever unapt was

174.2 and however // 146.20 and howsoever

174.3 Stratford. For the rest, he had sufficient money; // K:155.26 Stratford rather than Alcluid. He had money; // 146.21 Stratford-upon-Avon rather than to Alcluid. He had enough money now to make taxes an ever-present nuisance;

174.6 // 146.26 ¶Felix Kennaston

175.4 and speaking then of // 147.17 and to speak then of

176.2 notions as to the value of literature from a book. // 148.9 notions, as to the unimportance of books, from a book.

176.7 any how, // K:157.21 anyhow, // 148.14

176.17 // 148.24 ¶People

177.5 // 149.7 ¶Kennaston

177.7 and rational as // K:158.16 and as rational as // 149.8

177.16 a glance toward the sky the first clear night to show // 149.18 a glance toward the sky, after the falling of any reasonably clear night, to show

177.24 To his finicky love of neatness the universe showed // 149.25 The universe showed

178.2 There seemed so little harmony, so faint a sense of order, back of all // 149.27 There was no harmony, and no sense of order back of all

178.4 seemed just a jumble // 149.29 seemed to be just a jumble

178.24 ends. // K:160.1 ends, except—bewilderingly—when water froze. For then, as the microscope showed you, the ice-crystals were arranged in perfect and very elaborate patterns. And these stellular patterns, to the mused judgment of Kennaston, appeared to have been shaped by the last love-tap of unreason—when, in completing all, unreason made sure that even here the universe should run askew to any conceivable "design" and lose even the coherency of being everywhere irregular. // 150.18

179.24 center; // 151.21 center, and the stomach appeared a sadly lopsided affair;

180.1 viscera; the two divisions of the brain did not correspond; there was nothing on the left side to balance the troublesome vermiform appendix on the right; // 151.22 viscera: all the internal organs of the human body seemed to have been thrust in as promiscuously as though this bag of flesh were a hand-bag packed at train-time in wild haste. Then, also, the two divisions of the brain

180.11 // 152.8 ¶Nowhere

181.8 well-plotted // 152.28 well plotted,

181.11 *milieu* // K:162.13 milieu // 153.2

181.12 // 152.4 ¶Kennaston

181.20 Artist certainly // 153.11 artist, certainly,

181.21 occupied; // 153.12 occupied,

182.10 // 153.25 ¶To believe

182.18 or at best // 154.3 or, at best,

182.19 pre-meditation // K:163.15 premeditation // 154.4

182.20 // 154.6 ¶Singly

182.20 earth—not even // 154.6 earth—and nowhere else, so far as man might judge, not even

182.23 and there it was apparent // 154.9 and upon earth this sense of proportion was apparent

182.24 Kennaston seemed // 154.10 Kennaston now seemed

183.2 —the earth // 154.13 —and the planet earth

183.3 now, // 153.14 at present,

183.4 a romance the God // 54.15 a romance which the God

183.18 // 155.1 ¶Indeed,
183.20 situation // K:164.13 "situation" // 155.4
184.13 indeed, // 155.19 by and by,
184.18 wrath to benevolence, // 155.24 wrath and benevolence,
185.7 // 156.7 ¶Since
185.17 and was pregnant with value only in that thereby the full extent // 156.16 and all the regretable events of our first Good Friday were of value only in that through them the full extent
186.4 // 156.28 ¶Just as
186.14 imposing: // 157.9 imposing;
186.20 having at last // 157.14 having, at last,
186.22 it was really as a proof of confidence in his Author's literary abilities that Felix Kennaston was presently confirmed at our little country church, // 157.16 it was as an expression of entire confidence in his Author's literary abilities that Felix Kennaston was now confirmed, at our little country church,
187.15 theorizing // 158.2 theorizing,
187.17 slovenliness—of shapelessness—which make his writings so admirable, here alluring // K:167.18 slovenliness and shapelessness—very easy to see just what makes the writings of Felix Kennaston most admirable—here alluring // 158.3
188.13 Thus, he too entered at last into that belief which is man's noble heritage. . . . // K:169.1 THROUGH such airdrawn surmises, then, as I have just recorded did Felix Kennaston enter at last into that belief which is man's noblest heritage. . . . // 159.1
188.6 métier," // K:169.6 métier," // 159.6
189.15 is at any rate // 160.6 is, at any rate,
189.20 romance, a character // 160.10 romance, you may remember, a character
190.5 For it may well be // 160.20 It very well may be
190.16 Mr. Charles H. Yale. . . . // K:171.7 the Charles H. Yale who catered to our boyhood with those spectacular diversions. . . . // 161.1
190.19 not—and reserving always a permissible preference for pleasant delusions. // K:171.7 not—reserving always a permissible preference for the illusion which seems the more pleasant. // 161.4
191.3 'the occult.' I don't // 161.12 'the occult.' . . . No, I do not
191.4 dictate via the Ouija board // 161.13 dictate, via the Ouija board,
191.8 tipping a table for me, you understand. . . . But I quite fixedly // 161.17 tipping a table about the room for my entertainment. That sort of thing is tosh . . . Yet I fixedly
195.8 "belles-lettres." // K:175.7 "belles lettres." // 165.7
195.12 emotions which it is the privilege of art to arouse—joys without any inevitable purchase-price, regrets // 165.11 emotions

which it is the privilege of art to arouse, and gained large-hearted joys without any inevitable purchase-price, and regrets
195.17 most engrossed // 165.16 quite engrossed
198.19 // 168.3 ¶He was quite
199.6 emotions lovers // 168.13 emotions which lovers
199.19 in part // 168.24 in particular
199.23 // 169.1 ¶For unfaithful
201.2 // 169.27 ¶And he would
201.9 Agnés Forey, // 170.5 Ida Vertrey,
201.14 // 170.10 ¶In memory
202.2 some one-else: // K:181.4 some one else: // 170.20 someone else:
203.24 // 172.6 ¶He looked,
204.21 // 172.27 ¶The two women
205.8 // 173.9 ¶And she promptly
207.6 His voice had quavered—not ineffectively, // K:185.16 His voice had quavered—had quavered in fact very nicely, // 174.24
208.20 whisper. // 176.2 half-whisper.
208.23 "I—I am afraid // K:186.27 "I am afraid // 176.5
209.13 importance that // 176.18 importance, that
210.5 however // 177.5 howsoever
211.4 the dream // 177.20 then the dream
212.13 hand?" says he. // K:190.7 hand?" // 178.29
212.20 such feats of manual activity. // 179.6 such small hints.
212.23 tolerable compass // 179.8 some tolerable compass
213.5 "Nay, but you will // 179.15 "Nay," Kennaston answered, "but you will
213.10 who regard expedients toward amending the quirks of fate with puritan disfavor. // K:190.27 who accord these expedients to amend the quirks of fate their puritan disfavor. // 179.20 who accord to these expedients for amending the quirks of fate their starched disfavor.
213.15 my breeches. // 179.26 my breeches and my codpiece.
213.18 in the world." // K:191.8 in the world's eye." // 179.28
213.19 // 180.1 The boy said:
214.7 // 180.13 The boy replied,
214.8 sir, but I // 180.14 sir," Kennaston cried out gaily, "but I
214.10 // 180.17 ¶So saying,
214.19 cockerel, surely this place // 180.24 cockerel," Kennaston replied, "this place
215.3 is there no business on your mind // K:192.11 is there on your mind no business // 181.3
215.22 as a man, // 181.21 as a boy,
217.11 ill-affected; and Berkeley, // 182.10 ill-affected," Kennaston found himself saying; "and Berkeley,

217.14 // 182.13 Cromwell replied:

218.16 // 183.11 ¶And with this

219.15 them. In // 184.4 them," Ettarre replied. "In

225.3 thought you were, // K:200.20 thought you to be, // 188.13

226.3 émigrants, // K:202.2 emigrants, // 189.3

226.4 Révolution // K:202.4 Revolution. // 189.4 Révolution.

227.3 showed without suspecting, // K:203.1 showed, without suspecting, // 189.20

227.12 however // 190.5 howsoever

228.6 to an earthly woman. // K:203.27 to any of our women. // 190.22

229.9 // 191.19 The girl replied:

229.11 that secret was discovered, // K:205.2 was discovered that secret, // 191.22

229.16 // 191.26 He said:

229.17 Ettarre . . . . Monsieur // K:205.7 Ettarre. Yes, it is perturbing to be assured I am only a garment which is sometimes worn by that Horvendile who is of the Léshy, and who shifts other puppets than I can imagine. For I am an overweening garment, Ettarre,—or rather, let us say, I flauntingly esteem myself a fine feather in the cap of this eternal Horvendile. So does it sometimes seem to my vainglorious self-conceit that even this demiurgic Horvendile and his Poictesme, and, for that matter, all the living anywhere in this world, are only the notions of a certain fat and flabby dreamer—" ¶"Nobody can think that, dear Horvendile, so long as he recalls the Sabbat—" ¶"Indeed, I am not likely to foreget the Sabbat. . . . Monsieur // 191.27 [same as Kalki until 192.12 where read "Indeed," said Kennaston, in startled haste, "I am not likely to forget the Sabbat. . . .Monsieur

229.24 has been guilty in his career // K:206.1 has in his career been guilty // 192.20

230.7 goat, // K:206.8 Goat, // 192.26

230.9 is—and how // 192.28 is," the girl replied,—" and how

230.11 "Yet—even now // 193.1 "Yet—in despite of that which the Sabbat revealed,—even now

231.4 me // 193.17 me,

231.20 and how // 194.2 and saw how

235.11 only that dead horrible mangled worm, born dead, // 197.21 only that horrible, blue, smashed and bleeding thing, born dead,

236.6 Morsokoi, // 198.10 Morsokoï,

237.5 whatever I have done or learned or dreamed, // 199.3 whatever I have done or studied or dreamed,

237.8 odd. For all which has known life must suffer death." // K:212.16 odd, because we have both learned—by how many countless attestings!—that all which has known life must suffer death." // 199.6

237.17 A woman stood there, who did not speak, but only waited. At length he know what terror was, for terror possessed him utterly; and yet he was elated. // 199.15 ¶Moreover a woman stood there who did not speak, but only waited. So did he perceive what terror was, for terror possessed him utterly; and yet he was elated, in the while that he said,—

237.23 And Ettarre's hands, // 199.21 Then Ettarre's hands,

238.9 hackneyed crude misleading // 200.2 hackneyed, crude, misleading

238.10 woman he had loved she came, now that he was age-stricken and nearing death, for in this one dream alone // 200.3 woman whom the king had loved, and must love forever, that Ettarre had come, to guide him tenderly out of his kingdom in this world, now that the king was age-stricken and near to death, for in this one dream alone Kennaston

238.14 sure; the broken dream had remained an enigma; but he // 200.9 sure. The broken dream remained an enigma. But he

238.17 emotion: // 200.12 emotion;

240.7 // 202.1 Mrs. Kennaston observed, with a bright smile,

241.24 and—" // 203.12 and the very first evening—" ¶"No, dear, it was in the morning," my wife corrected me, "and everybody knows that the upstairs-girl everywhere used to help out with the cooking quite regularly—" ¶"Of course they did," Mrs. Kennaston remarked, with unconcealed indignation. "But now, even with the politest of them, you simply never know where you are. For what with the way they leave you, without one minute's notice, hag-ridden, Mr. Harrowby, is really not any name for it. They must go!"

243.5 recollect now // 204.19 recollect, now,

243.8 // 204.22 I replied:

243.15 Good Friday," // 204.28 Good Friday night,"

243.20 feasting, // 205.5 feasting, with somewhat unusual fare,

243.24 and when—when // 205.9 and—when

244.5 and certain portions // 205.13 and portions

250.14 country—very far from Lichfield— // 212.7 country, very far from Lichfield,

254.10 heaps, suggestive // 215.9 heaps suggestive

255.6 // 215.24 ¶Then he walked

255.24 matters with them. . . . // 216.15 matters, with them. . . .

256.2 which figures in my book, // 216.17 which figured first in *The King's Quest*, and which later came to be the gist of all my books,

256.23 People do not think much // 217.8 People do not think very much, nor at all clearly,

260.2 and hopeful that this much allusion at least was permitted // 219.19 and hopeful that they were at least permitted this much of allusion

260.6 as with indifference— // 219.23 as with entire indifference,—

262.4 Thereafter Felix Kennaston, as the world knows, wrote no more books, save to collect his later verses into a volume. "I am afraid to write against the author of *The Tinctured Veil*." // K:233.4 ¶Thereafter Felix Kennaston wrote no more books. He revised painstakingly, for the uniform edition of his works, the "privately printed" volumes of his remote youth; he collected a body of miscellaneous verse in the curiously unequal *Chimes at Midnight*: but after *The Tinctured Veil* he wrote nothing more save only those occasional papers which later were assembled in *How Many Angels*. "I am afraid to write against the author of *Men Who Loved Alison*," // 221.4 [no new ¶ 221.4 Read:. . . . And thereafter etc.

262.11 // K:233.16 ¶For this Kennaston to us seemed like an instrument that has been used to accomplish a needed bit of work, and, when the work was done, had been put by. And he did not matter: what only mattered was the fact that we possessed *Men Who Loved Alison*. A quota of youngsters here and there, I know, begin to assert that we have in *The Tinctured Veil* an affair of even more grave importance, and they may be right. It is a question which will for our generation remain unsettled. // 221.16 ¶For this Kennaston, to us, seemed etc. as in Kalki

262.12 Meanwhile, // 222.5 MEANWHILE,

262.17 Club, was // 222.10 Club, he was

263.15 And // 222.26 AND

264.5 who dared at outset marry his puppets, to each other, and tell you how their love remained unchanged. // 223.11 who dared at outset to unite his chosen pair of puppet lovers,—I mean, in plain prosaic marriage, with each other,—and then to depict their love as surviving their union, unchanged.

264.17 outrageous as // 223.24 outrageous, as

265.18 // 224.18 back* *one preserves with vast pleasure this archaic quaint touch.

265.20 —and in fine, // K:237.2 —and, in fine, // 224.20

266.9 and that common // K:237.14 and this common // 225.4

266.23 you can always hear at will o'nights? // K:238.1 you are privileged, now, to hear every night until the one or other of you is done with breathing? // 225.18

267.8 Felix Kennaston. // K:238.10 Felix Bulmer Kennaston. // 225.27

267.8 Concerning all of us, // K:238.10 Of all of us, // 225.27

267.15 me or // 226.4 me, or
267.16 notion— // K:238.17 notion,— // 226.5 [This is an exception. Usually Cabell has not added a comma before the dash in the Kalki edition.]
267.18 For all of us // 226.7 For each and all of us
268.1 which is not merely human // 226.12 which is not ever to be measured by the strait tenets of common-sense
268.2 however // 226.15 howsoever
268.5 not a futile // 226.17 not merely a futile
269.13 // 227.14 ¶So she kissed
271.15 this-or-that // 229.5 this or that
273.1 trivial bright object // K:243.17 small bright object // 230.8
274.13 // 231.14 ¶P. N. Flaherty
276.4 I found // 232.22 ¶In brief, I found
277.15 // 233.26 ¶Then he was silent. Evening was approaching now, and twilight gathered in the room. But as Kennaston sat there looking down into the open fire, its glow made plainly visible his pudgy and vacuous face. . . .
279.16 me that // 235.19 me, as we sat together there in the firelight, with the dusk rising everywhere about us, that
279.17 All I // 235.22 All which I
280.4 is not // 236.3 is not, not merely,
280.9 The man was not merely very human; he was humanity. And I reflected that it is only by preserving faith in human dreams that we may, after all, perhaps some day make them come true. THE END // 236.8 This man was not only very human: he was humanity.
237 of Storisende THE EPILOGUE The epilogue starts with the lines omitted: AND yet, sir," I had said, by and by, "yet it is only by preserving faith. . . . etc. as on p. 280 of First Edition.